"You have two minutes to tell me why you're here before I call the sheriff. And I'll shoot you in the foot if I don't like what you have to say."

Ewen had the audacity to grin. "Could you at least lower your weapon? I don't know what's going on at your home, but I'm totally innocent."

Tempe hesitated but lowered the rifle. "Said the spider to the fly," she mumbled.

"I heard that," he said and laughed.

Before she had a chance to take issue with him, Kylo bounded back into the barn and growled at Ewen. Ewen took a few steps back and Tempe was glad of it. Kylo quieted, raised his head and gave two short barks, causing Tempe to scan the farthest corners of the darkened barn. Kylo's ears lifted and, combined with her own gut feeling that something was off, that was good enough for her.

She moved forward, grabbed Ewen by the arm and started running toward the front door of the barn. "Something's wrong. We have to get out of here. Now!"

Liz Shoaf resides in North Carolina on a beautiful fifty-acre farm. She loves writing and adores dog training, and her husband is very tolerant of the amount of time she invests in both her avid interests. Liz also enjoys spending time with family, jogging and singing in the choir at church whenever possible. To find out more about Liz, you can visit and contact her through her website, www.lizshoaf.com, or email her at phelpsliz1@gmail.com.

Books by Liz Shoaf

Love Inspired Suspense

Betrayed Birthright
Identity: Classified
Holiday Mountain Conspiracy
Texas Ranch Sabotage

Visit the Author Profile page at Harlequin.com.

TEXAS RANCH SABOTAGE

LIZ SHOAF

LOVE INSPIRED SUSPENSE

INSPIRATIONAL ROMANCE

LOVE INSPIRED® SUSPENSE
INSPIRATIONAL ROMANCE

PLEASE RECYCLE
THIS PRODUCT IS RECYCLABLE

ISBN-13: 978-1-335-72244-7

Recycling programs for this product may not exist in your area.

Texas Ranch Sabotage

Love Inspired
22 Adelaide St. West, 40th Floor
Toronto, Ontario M5H 4E3, Canada
www.Harlequin.com

Printed in U.S.A.

He that is faithful
in that which is least is faithful also in much:
and he that is unjust in the least is unjust also in much.
–Luke 16:10

To Tempe Shoaf. One day I *will* finally get to meet you.

And I'd like to thank Jane Brightwell for graciously allowing me to use a fictional version of her dog in my book. He is, of course, much better trained than his fictitious counterpart. And thank you, Jane, for being the kindest dog-training partner ever.

ONE

Tempe Calloway's eyes flew open and her heart hammered in anticipation the moment the trip wire alert buzzed in her darkened bedroom. She'd been sleeping fully clothed every night for the past two weeks, waiting for this moment. Adrenaline spiked through her system as she scrambled out of bed, tugged on her boots and slipped the strap of her granddaddy's old Winchester rifle over her head and across her shoulder on the way out.

She peeked into Riley's room and checked that her eight-year-old daughter was safe and fast asleep, then motioned to Kylo, the solid black Australian shepherd lying on the end of Riley's bed. The young fifty-pound dog, who had come instantly alert, quietly jumped off the bed and followed Tempe down the stairs, close on her heels, as they silently slid out the kitchen door. She was well pleased when the dog-in-training followed her orders as they stayed right by the house, then ducked behind several trees on the way to the barn.

Holding the rifle loosely at her side, she plastered herself against the rough outer wall of the barn. Fury tore through her at the thought of another "incident" at the ranch, but she took a deep breath and waited. No one had any business skulking around the area so late at night, and now she finally had a chance to catch whoever had been causing all their recent problems—expensive problems they could ill afford.

She heard a few horses snort and rustle around inside their stalls as if disturbed, and it was all the information she needed. The large front doors of the barn were kept open during the heat of the summer and she quietly made her way around the rough-hewn structure, then slipped through the opening. Staying close to the wall, she allowed her eyes to adjust to the darkness and spotted a black-clad person furtively slipping out of the tack room.

Lips curling in a savage grin, Tempe lifted her rifle. Finally, she'd get some answers. "Stop, or I'll shoot."

The intruder's head whipped around, but that didn't help. Even through the darkness she spotted the ski mask covering the person's face and identity. A split second later, the figure stood still at the sound of Kylo's low snarl and then took off toward the side door of the barn. Before she could take up the chase, another noise from the opposite direction had her whipping around, rifle at the ready. Her pulse beat rapidly and she took a deep breath, calming herself as she'd been taught during her military training.

Did the first guy have a partner? She calmly focused and tightened her finger on the trigger as she watched a man race through the front doors of the barn.

Kylo snarled again and Tempe spoke in a low, firm voice, "Stop where you are, or I'll shoot."

He took her at her word and skidded to a stop. Before approaching him, Tempe gave Kylo a command, "Go round up the intruder, Kylo, I have this one." He was a natural in herding, even though he still tended to nip people in the behind to get them moving along. The dog took off, but she kept her eyes glued to the stranger.

Her gun still up and ready, she moved forward slowly, watching for any movement that would precede the drawing of a weapon. When she got close enough to see his face, she couldn't stifle her gasp of recognition.

The man wore a lopsided grin, and a lightning strike couldn't have been worse than the shock she received, but after the initial jolt, anger shot through her like a riptide. Anger that he might be responsible for the problems on the ranch, and another, more uncomfortable rage at her unfortunate attraction to this man.

She had deftly avoided him at his grandfather's castle in Scotland last December while searching for the map her granddaddy left her, but she'd been around him enough to realize her long-dormant heart had sprung to life. It wasn't going to happen. She wouldn't allow it with any man, not after what she'd been through, and especially not with the man standing in front of her. He was tall, around six feet four inches, with a runner's muscle mass. His wavy reddish-brown hair, combed straight back from his forehead, brushed the collar of his shirt. And those piercing blue eyes she remembered so well held a hefty amount of suspicion, and why was that?

"You!" she hissed through clinched teeth.

She lowered her rifle a few inches as a million questions sped through her mind. How had he found her? Did he know what she'd been after at his castle? Did he know about the map? Was he to blame for the things that had been happening around the ranch? Was he here to take the map back? That wasn't going to happen. She lifted the rifle back up and her finger tightened once again on the trigger. That map was rightfully hers, whether it proved to save the ranch or not.

"Hello, Maggie." He lifted a perfectly groomed eyebrow. "Or shall I call you Tempe?"

Busted! But it didn't matter. She had a solid reason for her actions in Scotland, and anyway, the man was up to no good, skulking around her barn in the middle of the night.

"You have two minutes to tell me why you're here before I call the sheriff. And I'll shoot you in the foot if I don't like what you have to say."

His gaze tracked her from her mussed-up bed hair to the soles of her worn-out boots. She tried not to let it affect her. She knew she looked a mess, but she stiffened her spine. She had only allowed a man to make her feel less than adequate one time in her life, and she was never repeating that nauseating experience.

He had the audacity to grin. "Could you at least lower your weapon? I don't know what's going on here at your home, but I'm totally innocent."

Tempe hesitated but lowered the rifle to her side. "Said the spider to the fly," she mumbled.

"I heard that," he said, and laughed insolently.

Before she had a chance to take issue with him, Kylo bounded back into the barn and growled at Ewen. Ewen took a few steps back and Tempe was glad of it. Kylo quieted, raised his head and gave two short barks, causing Tempe to scan the furthest corners of the darkened barn. Kylo's ears lifted, and, combined with her own gut feeling that something was off, that was good enough for her.

She moved forward, grabbed Ewen Duncan by the arm and started running toward the front door of the barn. "Something's wrong. We have to get out of here. Now!" she said loudly.

He resisted for a second, but then allowed her to pull him along. Her heart thundering in her chest, Tempe skidded to a stop twenty feet away from freedom when Kylo gave another two-bark warning. The dog lightly clamped his teeth on her arm and tugged her back toward the interior of the barn.

She glanced at the animal. "You sure?"

He tugged harder, and that was her answer. She jerked Ewen as best as she could—he was a large man—and headed back toward the stalls. She'd pray for safety if she still believed in God, but that ship had sailed a long time ago, after she was left on her own to raise a child. Since praying wasn't an option, she did her level best to get them to safety, because Kylo's two-bark warning meant—

The explosion at the front of the barn shook the old structure as if a hurricane had hit, lifted her off her feet and threw her forward through the air. Heat seared her back before she tucked herself into a ball and rolled as she hit the floor. Ignoring the light burning sensation on her back, she pulled herself up. The sight that met her eyes devastated her, but only for a moment. Large flames were devouring the entire front of the barn, and the hundred-year-old timber wouldn't last long. Her military training kicked in and she scrambled to her feet.

Spotting Ewen several yards away, she ran over to him and knelt by him. He was lying face down and shouldn't be moved, but there was no help for it. She had to get him out of there before they all burned up, and then there were the horses.

Kylo raced to her side, and she took a second to check him out. One small burn spot on his head, but otherwise he looked okay.

"Kylo, release the horses. You remember how, boy. We've been working on that trick."

The dog took off and Tempe rolled Ewen over, wincing at the redness on his face. He must have turned when the explosion ignited. He appeared to be close to two hundred pounds, but she was five feet ten inches herself and no lightweight. She didn't know the extent of his injuries, but thankfully, he seemed to be unconscious, because this might hurt, otherwise.

She lifted the gun strap over her head, and it settled across her shoulder. Squatting in front of him, she grabbed him by the waist and heaved him over her shoulder into a fireman's hold. She only wobbled a moment, then ran as fast as she could toward the open door.

Behind her the horses were screaming as Kylo

lifted the horse stall door latches with his nose. She had to move fast because the large animals would be bolting out of the barn right behind her.

When she staggered outside, one of the ranch hands came running up and helped her lay Ewen on the ground. He was beginning to come to, and she was glad he would be okay, but she turned and watched the last horse break free of the building just before the entire structure caved in on itself.

It was the last straw. Someone was going to pay for all the things happening at the ranch. She glanced at the man lying on the ground, coughing. Ewen Duncan better not be involved in this mess.

As awareness slowly crept in, Ewen became acutely conscious of a burning sensation on his face. He struggled to roll onto his side so he could stand, coughing several times as memories assailed him. He recalled the explosion and everything before, and then…nothing. This situation reminded him of a suspense scene in one of his novels and he quickly decided it was much more entertaining to write the scenes rather than live through them.

Two hands pushed him back down, returning him to his prone position on the hard-packed ground, and he glanced up, gazing into a pair of fierce green eyes. He couldn't believe the sweet, subdued librarian he'd met briefly at his grand-father's castle in Scotland was the same woman hovering over him. At the castle she'd dressed in dull shirts and skirts accompanied by an ugly tweed jacket. Her hair had always been scraped back into a tight bun, but now... Earlier, when entering the barn, he'd been stunned by the fe-rocious woman threatening his life with the rifle in her hand. Her hair was mussed and she was attired in old, raggedy jeans and a plaid shirt. She barely resembled the woman he'd met at the castle.

And she'd thrown accusations at him—some-thing about causing damage on her ranch.

He closed his eyes for a brief second, ques-tioning his sanity in tracking her down, but he didn't have an option. She had lied her way into his grandfather's castle under an assumed name and had been caught on camera stealing some-thing from the library. He needed to know what she'd taken.

Due to his dual citizenship and technology skills, the United States Defense Intelligence Agency had recruited him as an agent straight out of college, and the majority of his work was classified. Which presented a major problem. Tempe's actions reeked of deceit. Was she aware of his job with the DIA? Was she trying to steal data he'd analyzed? Had the castle been used as a drop-off and pickup location for the enemy, right beneath his nose?

He hadn't notified his superiors yet, didn't want to get her name placed on a watch list until he had answers. So he was here on his own time. Bottom line, he didn't trust her and was here to get answers, not answer them.

"Don't move. Bart went to the house to call Doc."

He opened his eyes and caught a flicker of sympathy in hers, but it dissipated quickly, replaced with the mistrust he'd been greeted with.

He raised a hand to touch his burning face and she gently knocked it away.

"Don't touch it until Doc gets here."

A sinking sensation filled his gut. "How did I get out of the barn?"

For the first time since he'd arrived at this desolate, parched piece of earth in Brewster County, Texas, near Big Bend National Park, Tempe Calloway grinned at him, and his stomach knotted.

"I carried you out."

His eyes still stinging from the smoke, he looked at her, scrutinizing her longer than he had during that brief moment in the barn. Her attire consisted of a faded Western-style shirt tucked into a pair of worn jeans. Scuffed cowboy boots adorned her feet and her long dirty-blond hair was pulled into a ponytail at the back of her neck. Instead of worrying about how he got to safety—an embarrassing thought—he addressed their current situation.

"Have you called the fire department?"

He followed her gaze toward the barn, and it was obvious the building couldn't be saved. There were several men valiantly trying to control the fire with water hoses, but it was a lost cause. At least the structure wasn't near any other buildings.

Ignoring her huff of disapproval, he rolled to his side and pushed himself off the ground. Doing a quick self-check, he determined the burn on his face was his only injury.

Straightening, he dusted himself off, glad he'd instructed Dudley, his valet, to purchase Western attire on his way to Texas. It was always a good idea to blend in, although the majority of his work took him to more sophisticated locales and people. He'd get a bath and change out of his regular clothes as soon as possible. He'd arrived at the ranch in the middle of the night to get the lay of the land, planning to present himself the following morning. He'd never expected to get caught, much less to become involved in a barn being burned to the ground.

Standing close to him with her arms crossed over her chest, Tempe snorted.

"What?" he snapped. He wasn't in the best of moods himself. After discovering her real name and locating her, he'd flown straight from Scotland, and then had to leave Dudley behind at the large airport to gather them a rental car while he took a rattletrap plane to a nasty little airport in Terlingua. He hadn't been aware that airports still had dirt runways. He'd hitched a ride from the airport so he could scout out Tempe's ranch without her knowledge. Well, the best-laid plans and all that.

She shook her head and her ponytail swung back and forth. "It's amazing. You just lived through an explosion and you still look like a *GQ* cover model. Don't you ever get dirty?"

Before he had a chance for a rebuttal, a middle-aged woman came rushing toward them from the direction of the house.

"Tempe, are you okay? What happened?" Her words held a combination of fear and anger. Ewen tended to pick up on nuances—it helped him develop characters in his books and also served him in his more clandestine work.

Tempe's face softened and his breath caught in his throat at the beauty she evidently took pains to hide, but then her face hardened.

"I'm fine, Aunt Effie, but whoever did this isn't gonna be fine when I catch up with them."

Effie looked as if she was about to say something, but firmed her lips and nodded toward Ewen. "Who is this?"

A myriad of emotions crossed Tempe's face before she answered. "This is Ewen Duncan. I caught him sneaking into the barn right before the explosion."

Her aunt's head snapped up. "You mean he's—"

"Yes, he's from Scotland," Tempe answered, cutting off whatever her aunt was about to say, arousing his curiosity.

Unspoken words passed from niece to aunt and Ewen's suspicions were ignited. These two women were up to something and he was determined to find out what. Tempe had stolen something and he wanted to know what it was. He couldn't fathom what a woman from Texas could want from a private castle library in Scotland, unless she was working for an enemy of the US.

"Is Riley still asleep?"

Riley? Ewen wondered. An accomplice? Before the older woman could answer, Ewen interrupted the conversation. The heat emanating from the burning building made his face hurt and he was exhausted.

"If I'm correct in understanding that someone set fire to your barn on purpose, then it stands to reason the perpetrator may still be on the premises. I suggest we go inside where it's relatively safe and sit down with a cup of tea."

While the two women were casting incredulous glances at his perfectly acceptable suggestion of tea, he slipped his hand into his pocket, wrapped his fingers around his cell and pressed a button he'd added to the side of his really, really smart phone, one he'd designed to his unique specifications. Based on Ewen's calculations, Dudley would see the alert on his own phone and should arrive within the next forty-five minutes.

Just then, a scream tore through the air from the direction of the house. A young girl came careening toward them, long dirty-blond hair flying behind her. It surprised Ewen how fast she reached them.

"Mama, there's a man in the house trying to break into the safe in Great-Grampie's office."

Tempe placed both her hands on the young lady's shoulders. Ewen noticed her fingers were trembling, but her voice stayed strong and steady as she looked her daughter in the eye. "Are you okay?" The girl nodded in the affirmative and Tempe took an awkward step back. It was obvious to Ewen just how shaken up Tempe was, but she put on a solid front and took command. "I'll handle this. Riley, you and Aunt Effie know what to do."

The understanding and old wisdom in Riley's eyes were way beyond what a child of that age should have, and Ewen stiffened in outrage. Just what was going on in this household?

"Yes'm," Riley said solemnly before taking Aunt Effie's hand. "Come get us when it's over."

Ewen watched Riley and Aunt Effie disappear behind the burning barn. "Where are they going?" he asked, unable to stop the accusatory tone in his voice.

Tempe's face hardened and her eyes narrowed. Ewen took a step back when she got in his face. "This is none of your business, Scottie Boy." Then her eyes narrowed. "Or it better not be."

After that ominous remark, Tempe lifted the rifle strap over her head and held the gun very comfortably in her hands, which wasn't completely surprising. While tracking her down, he discovered she'd been in the military, but he hadn't had time to do a deep search, which was rather unlike him. After learning she'd been working at the castle under an alias, he'd had a burning desire to confront her face-to-face, so he'd been on the move.

She turned toward the house and Ewen gently grabbed her arm to stop her, but she whipped around and knocked his hand off like it was a fly.

"Why don't you let your ranch hand take care of the intruder? Or better yet, wait until the police arrive?"

She gifted him with a grin that didn't denote happiness at all. The word that came to Ewen's mind was *feral*.

"Why don't you ask Bart?"

Ewen glanced at Bart, who appeared to be in his midfifties and had the physique of a lean, wiry cowboy. The man spit out a wad of tobacco, then said, "She's better trained than anyone on the ranch. Best let Tempe here handle whatever's going on."

When he turned back around, she had already slipped away. He caught a glimpse of a dirty-blond ponytail disappearing around the back of the house. He couldn't believe the men on this ranch were allowing her to risk her life, even if she did have some training. He didn't trust her, but he didn't want her killed. He held out a hand to Bart. "Give me the gun tucked inside your shirt."

Bart's eyebrows lifted in surprise and something akin to admiration shone out of his eyes. He slipped the gun out and handed it to Ewen butt first.

"Here ya go, but I think you'd be better off waitin' till she comes out. Tempe knows what she's doin'."

Bart drawled Tempe's name out and it sounded like Tempeee, heavy on the *e*. Ewen stored the information away and started running in the direction she had taken. He had just gotten to the back of the house when two gunshots pierced the still night air.

TWO

Tempe ducked as two bullets sped her way after she yelled down the hall for the intruder to stop. The figure, clad in black from head to toe, had fled her grandfather's office, and now she chased the person down the stairs. She almost caught up with them at the back door exiting the kitchen, but whoever it was could run like the wind. She lifted the old Winchester and aimed for a disabling shot, but the intruder turned and fired at her first. She had to duck back inside the kitchen for a second before taking aim once again. The person was too far away, but she fired anyway as they fled into the woods.

Frustration ate at her. A minute or two earlier and she would have cornered the perp in the office, but as she'd learned the hard way, what was done was done. Were they after the map she'd found in the book in Scotland? She kept it in the office safe. There was nothing else of value stored in there. She slumped against the wooden frame of the doorway and almost grinned when Ewen came careening around the corner of the house, but stood at attention when she spotted Bart's old gun in his hand, pointed straight in front of him.

Holding out a hand, she said, "Whoa, Scottie Boy, everything's okay. Lower the gun." She held her breath, but soon became impressed as he scanned the area, looking for potential danger. Not bad for a civilian.

He lowered his weapon to his side and stood there, staring at her. "Are you okay?"

Tempe shook her head and laughed. "Of course, I'm okay. I can't believe Bart parted with his pistol. It was a gift from his daddy, and he never lets anyone touch it." Tempe's fingers tightened on the Winchester when he stomped closer. She had no reason to trust a man who lurked around on her property in the middle of the night.

"You could have been killed," he snapped. "Do you always have to handle everything by yourself?"

Annoyance rippled through her. What she had to do, or not do, was none of his business. She moved forward, a breath away from a face too pretty for his own good. "I know what I'm doing, this is my ranch and you're trespassing. I want some answers."

He winced as he wiped his sleeve across his lips. Tempe almost felt sorry for him. Almost.

"Yes, well, I want some answers, too."

Hiding the fact that her traitorous heart was pounding from being so close to him, she nodded briskly. "Let's go round up the troops. I'll get Riley and Aunt Effie settled, then we'll talk."

He followed at her heels as she took long strides toward the burning barn. "What about the fire department and law enforcement? Did someone call them?"

Without breaking her stride, she shrugged. "Brewster County is large. I'm sure Bart called the sheriff, but it's a good ways to travel and he probably told him not to come until tomorrow morning, that we had the situation under control. People in our part of the country tend to take care of things themselves as much as possible."

He went quiet for a moment and she stopped and faced him, noting the thoughtful expression on his face.

"What?"

"You have quite a lot on your shoulders. You mentioned your grandfather's office. Do you and your husband, your daughter and your parents live here with him? Is this a family ranch?"

She shrugged and thought about her dwindling, but close-knit family. Aunt Effie, along with the ranch hands, held the ranch together and took care of Riley while Tempe served in the military. Tempe planned on mustering out when she finished her stint flying with the Blue Angels—if she was approved to rejoin for her last three months, but that was another story and she didn't have time to think about the crash right now.

"Not that it's any of your business, but they're all dead and Riley's father isn't in the picture. It's just me, Riley, Aunt Effie and the ranch hands living here on the ranch. I have a sister in New York." Dismissing him, Tempe stuck two fingers in her mouth and released a sharp whistle. A door opened from the ground beside another old building a safe distance from the barn.

Ewen made a strangling noise when Kylo flew upward as if rising from a grave and Riley and Aunt Effie followed.

"Were they hiding underground?"

The disbelief in his voice caused her to chuckle, something she hadn't done in a long while. "It's an old root cellar."

"Is it safe?"

Tempe stiffened at his sharp retort, which seemed to imply she didn't take care of her own. Riley and Aunt Effie came rushing toward them.

"Mama, I'm gonna go check on Buckeye, make sure he's okay."

Tempe grabbed the back of Riley's pajama top and pulled her back. "You, young lady, are going back to bed." She held up a finger, effectively stopping Riley's plea. "All the horses got out and Bart'll round 'em up and make sure they're okay."

Riley started to object and Tempe was pleased when she backed down.

"Let's all go to the house and get cleaned up. Whoever did this is long gone." At least that was what she hoped. It infuriated and scared her to the toes of her boots to think Riley had been in the house alone with an intruder. If anything like this ever happened again, she'd leave Kylo with her daughter.

She glanced at Ewen as dark suspicion filled her mind. "How did you get here? There's not a car in the drive." Before he could answer, a huge black car came careening down the dirt driveway, dust trailing behind it. She squinted in disbelief. Was that a full-sized limo? The light from the fire reflected off the long vehicle, confirming her suspicions.

"Is that a…?"

Ewen ignored her half question and started walking quickly toward the long black vehicle. Tempe, Riley and Aunt Effie followed close on his heels. Tempe lifted her rifle when the driver's door swung open and a vaguely familiar man immaculately dressed in a dark suit and multicolored tie scrambled out of the vehicle.

He glanced at the small group and Tempe stared at her aunt when the man's gaze lingered on the older woman. She was surprised to see the firelight reflect a blush on her aunt's face—Aunt Effie had always been such a practical, pragmatic woman.

His gaze quickly shifted back to Ewen. Concern filled his voice when the man asked, "Sir, are ye okay? I spotted the fire miles down the road." He moved closer. "Yer face looks a little red, if I may be bold enough to say so."

Tempe was fascinated by the interaction between the two men, but Ewen still hadn't answered her question.

"So how did you arrive if your—" she shot a hard look at the man about her aunt's age, who was driveling over Ewen "—driver just now got here?" It dawned on her that she'd seen him around the castle.

Ewen closed his eyes, blew out a breath, then opened them again. "This is Dudley. He, uh, traveled with me. He stayed in Midland so he could rent us a car while I chose to take a small plane. We checked and they didn't offer rentals at the Terlingua Ranch Airport. I wanted to get here as quickly as possible." He shot Dudley a hard look. "I requested a regular car, not a limo, which will stick out like a sore thumb in this area." He looked back at Tempe and she read the embarrassment on his face. "I, ah, shouldn't have arrived so early. A mechanic named Dewey, who works at the airport in Terlingua, gave me a lift here."

Tempe rocked back on her bootheels. "Uh-huh. You came to my ranch in the middle of the night to snoop. You never did answer my question. Why are you here?"

He raised his groomed brows. "I believe that answer lies with you. Tell me why you gained temporary employment under an assumed name at my grandfather's castle, and I'll be on my way."

Tempe huffed out a relieved breath when Dudley stepped forward and gave Tempe a half bow. "My proper title is actually valet to Master Ewen. I've been with him since he was a wee bairn in nappies."

Tempe almost laughed at the expression of horror that crossed Ewen's face, but her barn was burning down behind her and she had things to see to, mainly finding out who was trying to destroy her ranch.

"Where are you staying?" There wasn't a motel within a hundred miles. And there was no way they were staying at the ranch. *No way!*

Ewen stepped forward. "Dudley made arrangements for us to stay at a local guest ranch."

Dudley pointedly cleared his throat. "Sir, we left in a hurry, and all the way here, I did my best to locate accommodations, but wasn't able to find any."

Aunt Effie came to life and castigated Tempe. "Tempe, they can't go anywhere until Doc Hathaway arrives and checks out both of you, and it's the middle of the night. We have plenty of extra bedrooms and there are locks on the doors."

Before Tempe could intervene, Kylo, standing at her side, turned and released a low warning growl, causing Tempe to smoothly lift her rifle and spin toward the woods.

Ewen froze when Tempe raised her weapon and scanned the closest tree line through the scope. He didn't fully know what was going on yet, but for some strange reason he trusted her instincts.

"Aunt Effie, take everyone inside." She lowered her rifle as if everything was okay, but the tightness around her eyes told a different story. "I'll be along in a minute. I'm going to check the horses, make sure Bart has everything under control."

She and her aunt passed more unspoken words between each other before Effie smiled and took Riley's hand. "Come on, Riley. Let's get you back in bed and I'll put some coffee on for when Doc Hathaway gets here." Effie nodded at Dudley. "Grab your gear and we'll get you and your boss settled."

Ewen used his own unspoken words and tilted his head toward the women, instructing Dudley to follow them into the house and keep them safe.

After Ewen's grandfather insisted that Dudley accompany him on his many travels, Ewen had confided in his old friend about his role in the DIA. He really had no choice and he trusted Dudley implicitly. He was the only person, outside of Ewen's superiors, who knew Ewen worked for the agency. Dudley was a very fit fifty-five-year-old, and Ewen had to admit he had come in handy several times over the years. People tended to mistakenly—to their detriment—place Ewen in the pampered, rich guy category when they met his valet, until it was too late. Plus, as Dudley had so eloquently told the Calloways, he'd had been with Ewen since Ewen was in diapers.

"Kylo, stay with Riley," Tempe instructed, peering behind Ewen.

Ewen turned and spotted the animal. He was solid black, with different-colored eyes. One gold, the other blue. And it looked like the dog wanted to take a bite out of him.

Tempe chuckled. "You better keep a watch on Kylo. I'm training him, but herding comes natural to an Aussie. He'll nip you in the behind if you're not careful."

It sounded to Ewen as if Tempe wouldn't mind the dog nipping him. He watched as Kylo reluctantly obeyed Tempe and followed the troupe headed for the house.

"That goes for you, too, Scottie Boy. Go on to the house. I won't be far behind."

He ignored her command. "What did you see in the woods?"

"Just checking. It's dark, can't see much outside the firelight. Go on in, I'll be there shortly."

"I'm coming with you." He raised the gun in his hand. "I still have Bart's pistol."

She stared at him a minute, then shrugged. "Fine, but stay quiet and keep up. I thought I spotted movement in the woods. It could have been a coyote or bobcat, maybe even a black bear, but I want to be sure. Act natural and follow me."

She casually moved toward the front of the barn, then ducked low and ran through the darkness to the woods on the other side, with him just steps behind. Once they got there, he squatted down beside her.

Staying in the persona she believed him to be—wealthy and spoiled—he asked, "Do you have many wild animals in the area?"

It was too dark to see, but he heard the smile in her voice. "Don't worry, the fire likely scared off any lingering wildlife, which is why I wanted to check the perimeter before we settle in for the night. Now be quiet and keep up."

Staying in a crouched position, she slowly crept through the woods and Ewen was impressed at her stealth. Was that due to her military training, or had she been trained as a spy?

He slipped on a pair of special sunglasses that weren't available on the open market yet and scanned the surrounding area with the infrared lenses. They stayed low and moved through the scrub brush and trees. She held up a hand and knelt on her knees in the dirt. Ewen looked to where she was pointing. On closer inspection, he saw it—the slight imprint of a bootheel on the ground. The lady had a sharp eye. Too sharp? Especially out here in the dark. Just who was this woman, and what had he stepped into the middle of? Could the destruction of her ranch be retaliation from one of her enemies?

"He hasn't been gone long," she whispered without looking at him. "Could still be in the woods. I was sure whoever it was had left."

"Maybe the intruder came this way on his way out, hence the boot or shoe imprint left in the leaves."

They were squatting close together, whispering, and the moment felt way too intimate. "*Hence?* Nobody uses words like that," she said in a surprisingly teasing manner.

The smile slid off her face when she looked at him and noticed his glasses. "Why are you wearing sunglasses at night?"

Ewen spotted movement in the scrub brush behind her and whispered, "I'll explain later, but at the moment, we have company."

The muzzle of a rifle extended out of the scrub bush and Ewen threw himself on top of Tempe, pushing her to the ground as a muffled pop sounded and a bullet whizzed past.

THREE

Tempe hit the ground hard and Ewen landed on top of her, knocking the breath out of her lungs, but she was well trained and it didn't take but a few seconds to gather her wits.

"Position of the shooter?"

"Twelve o'clock, point of origin being the top of your head."

"You still have Bart's gun and I have my rifle. We're pinned down, so here's the plan. We come up shooting and create two targets. You peel off to the left and I'll go right."

"I have a better plan."

Tempe held back the sharp retort balanced on the tip of her tongue. She was the one with military training, not him, so she listened with impatience. The shooter could be circling around them, trying to find a better shot. They were sitting ducks.

"I have a small device in my pocket. It works like a flash-bang, but only produces an explosion of light when released, not the noise or danger. It won't stop the shooter, but it might scare them off."

Tempe was momentarily stunned. "Are you a James Bond junkie?"

She heard a very soft chuckle. "We're a real pair, aren't we? James Bond and Annie Oakley. To answer your question, let's just say I love technology. And to answer your earlier question, my sunglasses are infrared."

She ignored his poor attempt at humor and considered his plan. It was better than hers, she had to admit, but when they got out of this situation, she had a lot of questions, and if she didn't like the answers, well, she'd deal with it then.

"Okay, let's do it."

"Okay." She felt him digging around in his pants pocket, and then he barely whispered, "On the count of three I'll throw it at the last known position of the assailant and we wait and see if he makes a run for it. It's too dangerous to follow him in the dark in case there's more of them."

"I agree."

"One, two, three." Tempe felt his arm lift as he threw the modified flash-bang. He raised himself off her and they both scrambled to their knees as an explosion of light briefly lit up the area. Ewen pointed and they both watched as the shooter scrambled away and disappeared into the darkness.

She turned toward the ranch. "Let's get back to the house. I want to check on everyone."

Her thoughts running a mile a minute, Tempe stayed quiet and processed everything that had happened. There was more, much more, to Ewen Duncan than he presented to the world.

Both of them hoisted their weapons when they neared the house and found a car pulling into the driveway. Tempe lowered hers when she recognized the vehicle.

"That's Doc Hathaway. Let's go inside so he can check us over."

Following close on her heels toward the doctor's old Caddy, Ewen mumbled, "His name sounds like it came from an old Western movie. Wouldn't surprise me if he's ridden in on a horse."

That remark just burned, especially after the Annie Oakley comment. Tempe almost turned around and let him have it, but stopped herself. He'd learn soon enough about Doc Hathaway. Just to add fuel to the fire, she said, "Well, Doc has been known to hop on a horse and ride out to see to a ranch hand who got themselves into a spit of trouble while tending the cattle."

The engine cut off, and Doc flung open his door and unfolded his tall, elegant body from the driver's seat. His silver hair gleamed in the dwindling firelight from the burning barn as his gaze shifted from the destruction behind them and landed on Tempe and Ewen. A frown marred his forehead.

"More trouble, Tempe?" Doc asked in his sophisticated, cultured voice. "Have you called the sheriff?"

She couldn't help but slide a glance at Ewen, satisfied to see the stupefied expression on his face.

"Yeah. He'll come out tomorrow, but between the fire, the horses and the ranch hands, I expect any kind of evidence was destroyed. We found a partial shoe print and had a little trouble out in the woods, and I'll close off the office in the house until he gets here."

Doc's silver eyebrows rose. "The intruder entered the house? Is everyone okay?"

Tempe grinned because Doc just loved Riley to pieces. "My daughter is fine—" she turned grim "—but we'll have to be more vigilant until we catch whoever is doing this."

Doc turned toward Ewen and held out a hand. "Doc Hathaway."

Ewen shook his hand. "Ewen Duncan."

Doc's eyebrow rose again. "You wouldn't happen to be *the* Ewen Duncan? The famous novelist?"

Ha! Surprised again! Tempe thought with satisfaction. Doc was a well-read man.

"One and the same," Ewen said, and Tempe could tell by the tone of his voice that Doc had thrown him off-kilter because he didn't fit the mold Ewen had visualized.

"Nice to meet you. I have a dozen questions, as I'm sure most of your fans do, but I can see the redness on your face and we need to get you two inside to check you out."

They started walking toward the house and Doc continued, "Not that I'm a family doctor, just the closest medical person around here. The nearest doctor is about a hundred miles away. I'm retired, but when the locals call, I do what I can to help."

Ewen studied Doc Hathaway and Tempe could almost see that writer's curiosity eating away at his brain.

"Exactly what kind of doctor are you?"

Doc waved a negligent hand in the air. "Oh, I was in cardiology, practiced in Dallas until I retired and moved here to get out of the city. I always loved the country and open spaces and planned this move for many years. My wife passed away years ago and small-town life offers a sense of community and closeness that's hard to find in a large city. The church is the glue that holds the area together and people don't hesitate to help one another."

Tempe stayed quiet and followed both men up the front steps and onto the porch. Aunt Effie held the screen door open as they all filed in and made their way to the kitchen. Everyone took a seat around the old, scarred oak table and Doc Hathaway made short work of checking Ewen's facial burns.

"Nothing serious, just minor first-degree burns. A cool cloth on your face tonight along with some lotion and an over-the-counter pain reliever should do the trick." His silver brows lifted in admonishment. "But don't break the blisters if any should appear."

Tempe reveled in perverse pleasure to see Ewen take the doctor seriously after all but accusing him of being a cow-town doctor, but she sucked in a sharp breath of pain when Doc Hathaway lifted the back of her shirt after she told him where it was burning.

"Hmm. Not as bad as Mr. Duncan's here, but then he got a direct blast of heat. Do the same as I told him and you should be fine in a few days."

Weariness set in as she thought about everything she'd have to deal with in the morning. After rolling her shoulders to get the kinks out, she glanced at the multifunction watch she wore when flying with her Blue Angel team and saw it was three in the morning. All she wanted was a good night's sleep. She could question Ewen tomorrow.

Aunt Effie slipped from her chair and started gathering the coffee cups off the table. Tempe stood up with her.

"Leave everything until morning. It's time we all got some sleep. Doc," she said as she turned his way, "you're welcome to stay the night if you don't want to drive to your place."

Doc Hathaway rose from the table and smiled. "I appreciate the offer, but I always sleep better in my own bed. Call if you need me," he said, and let himself out.

Tempe waited to hear the rumble of his Caddy before motioning Aunt Effie and Ewen out of the kitchen. "Let's get some shut-eye. We can talk in the morning." And that was when she would demand some answers. Ewen looked as if he wanted to argue, but his lips firmed and he stayed quiet. Smart man. Tempe had had enough for one day.

He followed her around as she did a quick check, making sure all the downstairs doors and windows were locked, then motioned him ahead of her up the stairs. They were halfway up the steps when the sound of a caterwauling cat and a barking dog came from above them, and she briefly wondered if this horrific day would ever end.

* * *

Ewen closed his eyes against a bombardment of embarrassment and anger. He was going to kill Dudley. Laying a hand on her arm to keep her from rushing to investigate, he gave Tempe a sheepish look. "I know what made that horrific, screeching noise. It's Simba. He's a very bossy and opinionated tabby cat. I assume Dudley somehow smuggled him on this trip."

Before Tempe had a chance to respond to his explanation, the noise upstairs erupted into total chaos. Sharp barks were accompanied by Simba's shrieking, and they were almost knocked down the stairs when Simba came careening around the corner of the hall with Tempe's dog scant inches from her tail. Tempe moved so fast that if Ewen had blinked he would have missed her catching the dog by the collar and calling a stop to the chase.

"Kylo, halt!"

To Ewen's amazement, the dog focused totally on Tempe and ignored Simba's taunt at the bottom of the stairs.

With her hand on Kylo's collar, she shot Ewen a smug look. "You need to control your cat."

Ewen took issue with the challenging glint in her eye, then made the mistake of looking down at the large tabby, who seemed to be daring anyone to tell him what to do. He was saved the humiliation of having to chase the beast all over the house when Dudley and Riley skidded to a stop at the top of the steps.

Ewen blinked rapidly in more mortification when he saw Dudley's pajamas. The top and bottom were red-and-gray plaid, the Duncan tartan colors. A duplicate of the tie his valet had worn earlier.

"Dudley, see to the cat. Tomorrow we'll discuss how he came to be here."

Dudley met him on the stairs. "I apologize for the intrusion of the castle pet, sir, but I just couldn't bear to leave him behind."

Ewen was surprised when Tempe shrugged. "It's just a cat."

A giggle at the top of the stairs had him lifting his head. It was Riley, whose gaze was following Dudley as he attempted to corral Simba. She lifted two fingers to her mouth and released a shrill whistle. The monstrous cat lifted his head, then proceeded to streak up the stairs, right past the dog and straight into Riley's arms. She cooed and rubbed the big tabby's head.

"Mom, you take Kylo. Simba can stay with me tonight."

Tempe gave her daughter a nod and Ewen marveled again at the striking resemblance between mother and daughter. Dudley trudged back up the stairs, and Ewen and Tempe parted to allow him through.

"If you'll follow me, sir, I have your room ready."

If the floor had opened up and swallowed him whole, it would have saved him the embarrassment of Tempe hearing his room had been readied for him. But the most extraordinary thing happened—Tempe half grinned, revealing two delightful dimples. His heart skipped a beat at the sight, but he straightened his bearing. There was no way he was getting involved with a possible thief and traitor. He had to maintain his distance. Plus, due to his family's wealth and his own high profile, many women had tried to manipulate him into marriage. He didn't trust most women's motives.

Without making a comment, he followed Dudley up the stairs. His valet led him through the third door on the right. He took in the room. It was very clean, but similar to the exterior of the house, it had a shabbiness he attributed to lack of funds. His gaze moved from the picture on the wall depicting a herd of buffalo running across a plain, to his pajamas laid neatly on the side of the bed awaiting him, and he thought about Tempe.

She felt like a breath of fresh air compared to most of the people he'd been exposed to lately. Yes, he was attracted to the woman, but looks could be deceiving, and the majority of the time they were, at least in his line of work at the DIA. He moved into the room and Dudley left with a quiet snick of the door behind him. He picked up his pajamas and sternly reminded himself he had a lot of questions for Tempe, the main one being, what did she steal from the castle library? The evidence was clear on the video he'd reviewed. Cameras were a friend to a man who'd made a career in intelligence, and he'd installed them all over the castle.

He quietly changed into his pajamas, slid his feet into the slippers sitting on the floor and searched for the adjoining bathroom, but came up empty. He was tired and cranky after the long flight from Scotland. His face hurt from the minor burn, and he wasn't happy that his valet had brought the cat and failed to explain the bathroom situation.

Slipping out of his room into the quiet hall, lit only by a few night-lights plugged into electrical sockets low on the wall, he proceeded forward in search of the facilities. He assumed the master bedroom had its own bathroom and the rest of the bedrooms shared one. He spied a door at the end of the hall and started in that direction, but stopped when he heard a door opening and closing at the bottom of the stairs.

After what had transpired earlier, he went on

high alert. Had someone broken into the house? He didn't want to scare anyone, but the household needed to be alerted immediately.

Taking a deep breath, he yelled at the top of his lungs. "There's an intruder in the house."

A minute later, doors up and down the hallway were flung open. Wearing rumpled pajamas, her hair in a tangle, a white-faced Tempe ran out of a room two doors down and across the hall from his. She searched the hallway, then zeroed her focus on the door next to his.

"Riley," she breathed, before running to the door and wrenching it open. Ewen stumbled in after her, only to find a disgruntled Simba pacing across the bed, alone. Riley was nowhere to be seen.

FOUR

Fear gripped Tempe's belly and almost choked off her air when it rocketed upward and lodged in her throat. Riley was the most precious thing in her life and she wasn't in bed, where she was supposed to be. Taking a deep breath, Tempe forced herself to calm down and think. She whirled around and bumped into Ewen's chest. With a quick step back, she raised her chin, doing her best to hold herself together.

"Did you see an intruder, or just hear something?" Her voice barely wobbled. When he didn't respond, she asked more forcefully, "Ewen, answer my question. Now!"

He tore his gaze from Riley's empty bed and shook his head. "Sorry, I was trying to locate the facilities and heard what sounded like a door closing downstairs."

Tempe sorted through the information and remembered Riley being worried about Buckeye. The Thoroughbred was not only valuable, Riley loved him, and naturally, after the fire, she'd be worried about him. The thought calmed her, but after the barn fire and other incidents, it was too dangerous for an eight-year-old girl to be roaming around in the middle of the night, especially with a shooter unaccounted for.

Shoving Ewen out of the way, she skidded to a stop in the hall. She wasn't used to having so many people in her house, and at any other time, the scene in front of her would have been humorous. Dudley, decked out in plaid pajamas the same color as the tie he'd worn earlier, stood beside Aunt Effie, who was attired in sensible pajamas. Dudley looked confused and Aunt Effie stared at her until Tempe explained.

"Nothing to worry about. Y'all go on back to bed. I'm pretty sure Riley went to check on Buckeye." Taking no more time to reassure them, Tempe motioned Kylo to follow her. She quickly slipped her boots on in her bedroom, slid a knife into one boot, grabbed the rifle she'd brought up earlier and flew down the stairs, jerking open the front door.

She headed toward the training ring where Bart would have corralled the horses. When she arrived with Kylo at her heels, she desperately searched the ring of horses. There stood Buckeye, off to one side, but her daughter was nowhere to be seen. Ewen came up beside her, and for the first time in years, she was glad for the company, and to not have to handle this alone.

"They got her, I know it," she whispered, her hands trembling on the rifle.

In a clipped tone she'd never heard from him before, Ewen said, "We don't know that, but if it's true, we'll find her."

The sheer command and confidence in his voice reassured her. She had always been so independent, taking care of everything herself, but this time was different. This time the thing she loved most in the world was at risk. Shaking her head, she pulled herself back together. Standing there, allowing terror to fill her, wouldn't help to locate Riley.

"Kylo, find Riley."

Ewen moved to the side when the dog started sniffing the ground. Riley had spent a lot of time in the practice ring, and it took him several minutes to trace the scent where it left the area. When he followed it out of the ring and toward the scrub brush, he sat down with his ears up, face pointing toward the open pastures.

Tempe released the breath she was holding. She'd been training Kylo to track, but didn't know if he fully understood the concept yet. "Go," Tempe commanded, and Kylo took off.

It was all they could do to keep up with the dog's speed, but Tempe was prodded by sheer fear for her daughter. She tore through large white-brush bushes, their thorns tearing at her clothes, but nothing mattered except finding her daughter.

Kylo had been learning to track without barking, so if someone had Riley, hopefully they could approach without being heard. As soon as they cleared the brush into an open area, she saw the dog had stopped, ears up, facing a small cave—one of many scattered throughout the foothills standing sentinel at the base of the massive Chisos Mountains, which were still a good distance away.

She took a deep breath to slow her racing heart and control the chilling thoughts crowding her mind, and became aware of Ewen standing quietly at her side.

"Do you think she's in there?" she barely croaked out, hardly able to speak past the panic clogging her throat.

He placed a hand on her shoulder and warmth permeated through her shirt. She ignored the small flash of attraction. Now was definitely not the time to be concerned about that.

"I think there's a good chance, but we have to be careful. Can your dog get closer and give us any indication of what's going on in the cave?"

She blew out another breath. *Think!* She had to stay calm and think. "Yes, at least I hope so. Kylo, scout," she commanded.

He crouched low and circled to the right, coming up parallel to the cave. Tempe held her breath as he ever-so-slowly approached the cave and peered in. She readied her rifle when Kylo released a big bark and flew into the cave.

"Go! Go! Go," she shouted and started sprinting forward. She had no choice but to run straight into the opening. She was ready to shoot, but it took a minute to get her bearings. Kylo was hovering protectively over a small huddled form curled up in a corner of the cave. Tempe lowered her rifle—there was no one else in the cave or Kylo would have been frantically barking. She approached her dog and the small bundle lying close to him, her heart literally in her throat. Was her daughter alive?

She sensed Ewen by her, but she was so focused on Riley she barely felt him touching her arm again. She nudged Kylo aside, touched the pulse at the base of her daughter's neck and heaved a sigh of relief when she felt a strong, pounding heartbeat.

She blinked rapidly when Ewen flicked on a flashlight and pointed it toward Riley. Her daughter's feet and hands were bound, and a wide piece of tape covered her mouth, but it was the fire in Riley's eyes that told Tempe her daughter wasn't injured, just good and mad.

Pulling the KA-BAR out of her boot, she cut

the bindings on Riley's hands and feet, then slowly pulled the tape off her mouth. Her daughter's temper flared and that, more than anything, reassured Tempe that everything was going to be okay.

"Mama, I'm spittin' mad. I went out to check on Buckeye—I know I wasn't supposed to—but those two men grabbed me. I told 'em you'd shoot their boots off if they so much as hurt a hair on my head, and I told them if they didn't let me go, you'd track them down like rabid animals. That's when they slapped the tape on my mouth, but I got a few good kicks in before they put the tape on my hands and feet."

Tempe just folded Riley into her arms and breathed in the essence of her daughter. She was okay. Riley was okay. Ewen squatted down beside them and Tempe reluctantly released her daughter.

"Riley," Ewen asked, "did they hurt you in any way?"

Tempe choked back a semi-hysterical laugh when Riley scrunched up her nose. "Naw, right after they grabbed me, I heard one of 'em say they weren't to hurt anyone, just put a scare into 'em. That's when I knew everything would be okay." She turned to Tempe. "I knew you would find me, Mama. I wasn't too awfully worried." But Riley's trembling lips and earnest expression told the truth. Her daughter was more shaken up than she was letting on. "I'm sorry, Mama, I know I shouldn't have gone out on my own, what with everything going on at the ranch, and I promise it won't happen again."

"I'm just glad you're okay. Let's get back to the house," Tempe said, her own lips trembling with relief.

Riley scrambled to her feet and dusted off her jeans. As they started the long trek back to the house, Tempe questioned Riley about her two kidnappers. They were outfitted in Western wear, but bandannas covered their faces. The only information of any significance was that one of them had a beard and they didn't seem ill at ease on a ranch. Tempe listened carefully to her daughter, but she stayed ultra-vigilant to their surroundings, all the time wondering why these men went to the trouble of kidnapping her daughter, only to leave her tied up in a cave on the ranch. Was it meant to be a warning of some kind?

When they got back to the house, Ewen was relieved that everyone appeared to be in bed. They must have taken Tempe's assurance to heart that everything was okay. Tempe gave him a curt nod. "I appreciate the help. I need to talk to my daughter."

Ewen took the hint and said good-night to

both ladies, but at the top of the stairs, he ducked around the corner and stopped to eavesdrop. He didn't trust Tempe, but found himself intrigued by both her and her courageous daughter.

"M-Mama, I'm sorry I left the house without permission. It won't happen again."

Ewen heard the child's voice wobble and his heart clenched.

"I know you said we might have to sell Buckeye if we can't raise enough money to keep the ranch in the black, and I know I pitched a fit about keeping him." Ewen heard a loud sniffle before she continued. "But he could have been hurt in the fire tonight, so I wanted to tell you it's okay if you sell him, so long as he gets a good home."

Ewen held his breath, his heart in his throat, waiting to see how Tempe would respond to this heartfelt plea.

"Come here, baby," Tempe said, her voice softer than he'd ever heard it. "First of all, let's get one thing straight. We're never selling Buckeye."

"But Mama, what if he gets hurt?"

"I won't allow that to happen, and I'm going to stop whoever's doing these things on the ranch." She paused. "Riley, I don't like you having to grow up so fast. At your age, you shouldn't be worried about whether we'll lose the ranch. Listen, I want you to know I'm proud of you. It took courage to go through what happened tonight."

Ewen strained to hear Riley's whispered response.

"I asked God to help me and He did. He sent you and Mr. Duncan to find me."

"That's good, baby, but with everything going on, I think it might be a good idea for you and Aunt Effie to visit your aunt Liv in New York for a little while."

"Mama, you taught me how to shoot and ride. I can take care of myself."

An eight-year-old taught to shoot a gun? Ewen's sympathy for Tempe somewhat lessened. Yes, they lived in the country, but such a young girl with a gun in her hand was hard for him to imagine.

"And besides, Aunt Liv's apartment is hardly big enough for a person to turn around in. You said so yourself. There's only one bedroom and we can't afford a hotel room."

"Fine, but if you stay here, we're going to have a few new rules, one of them being no sneaking out at night. We'll have someone keeping watch at all times. You head on up to bed and get some sleep. It'll be morning before we know it and tomorrow's going to be a long day."

"School's out for the summer and I can pick

up more chores," Riley said, a smile in her voice as she pounded up the stairs.

Ewen ducked into the shadows as she ran past him, straight into her room, and shut the door.

"You can show yourself now, Scottie Boy," came an irritated voice from the bottom of the stairs.

Ewen walked down the steps, stopping in front of Tempe. "Do you really think it's a good idea to teach a little girl to handle a gun?" A flash of anger flared briefly in her eyes, but then her expression went blank. He much preferred the anger.

"Not that it's any of your concern, but I'll answer your question. When you grow up on a ranch, it's better to teach the young ones to respect guns, and the proper way to handle them, because just about every cowboy on the property carries one. There are all kinds of threats, from coyotes to bears, and everyone has to be prepared. Did I teach my daughter how to handle a gun? You betcha' I did. I also put her on a horse when she was three years old. If you have a problem with that, you're welcome to leave tomorrow morning. Come to think of it, I don't know why you're still here."

His anger lessened because he realized she was right, but he was tired and grumpy and shot back, "You know why. I want to know what you were doing at the castle library under an assumed name." He hesitated, then added, "There's a camera installed inside the library. Video doesn't lie. You stole something from one of the books, and I want to know what it is." He hadn't hidden information in a book, but he suspected that somewhere along the way, someone had, and she could have been sent in for a retrieval.

She ignored his comment, brushed past him and started walking up the stairs. "Why don't we get some rest and we'll discuss your stay in the morning."

She disappeared into her bedroom and left him standing there.

"Who are you, Tempe Calloway, and what's your story?" he mumbled as he climbed the stairs himself, heading straight for the facilities. Ten minutes later, he lay in his bed, staring into the darkness. A ton of questions peppered his inquisitive brain. Why was the ranch in financial trouble and who had something to gain by making sure it stayed that way? And then there was Tempe herself. She was definitely physically fit. The word *beautiful* could also be applied, but he shied away from that description. She was also overlaid with a hefty dose of confidence, probably due to her military training.

It had been a long time since anything really challenged him, and the mystery shrouding

Tempe, along with the happenings at the ranch, were definitely a challenge. How was her time at the castle in Scotland connected to current events, because the tingle at the back of his neck told him it was, and he was on the precipice of discovering the truth.

He grinned in the dark. Added to that, Tempe didn't even remotely go out of her way to attract his attention—quite the opposite, in fact—and perversely, that intrigued him even more, in a personal way. The woman had a trunk full of secrets and he found himself itching to expose all of them.

Yes, he thought as he drifted to sleep, he was definitely sticking around.

Maybe he shouldn't stick around after all. The next morning, with no opportunity to question her further, Ewen found himself sitting in a truck staring at a decrepit helicopter that appeared as if it was on its last legs. Earlier, during a hearty, satisfying, ranch-style breakfast of steak, eggs, biscuits and gravy, it wasn't the proper time, with everyone listening at the table, to interrogate Tempe. Instead, Ewen had done his best to convince Tempe he could help catch the perpetrators attempting to destroy her ranch. She had no idea just how qualified he was to handle that. He had to convince her to allow him and Dudley to stay at the ranch. That would give him plenty of time to find answers.

Aunt Effie had shot him a pitying look, and he hadn't quite trusted Tempe's grin when she gifted him with a big, wide Texas smile and said, "Okay, Scottie Boy, let's see what you've got."

She'd commanded Kylo to "stay," and Ewen had followed her outside to a rusted-out truck that belonged in a junkyard. She'd driven them to a field where several tumbledown buildings held sentinel. And now his stomach dipped while he sat there, staring at the helicopter squatting in the middle of them like a small, hulking beast.

She turned the truck engine off and sat there, both hands on the steering wheel. "Listen, Ewen, I appreciate your offer to help and everything, but you're out of your element here. Why don't you just head on back to Scotland where you belong?"

Praying they weren't going to ride in that death trap sitting in front of them, he stiffened his back. "Why don't you tell me what you took from the castle library, and I'll be on my way."

Her hands gripped the steering wheel and the tingling in his neck increased. She opened her mouth, then closed it. "Fine. I'm going to do a flyover and check the herd and pastures, make sure our late-night visitors didn't do any more damage." The driver's door creaked ominously when she threw it open. Sticking her head back in, she grinned, and his challenge meter went on red alert. "That's if you're game."

Definitely a challenge. He glanced at the helicopter. He'd experienced quite a few dicey situations during his tenure at the DIA, but that machine looked to be on its last legs. It used to be green, based on the patches of paint still attached. The red lights protruding from the front and sides made it look like something out of a comic strip. And what was that oblong object attached to the side?

"How old is that thing and who's going to fly it?"

Her grin widened. "I am. And not to worry, I bought it at a boneyard, so it might be old, but I'm a fairly decent mechanic. I fixed 'er right up."

The dare to climb into that death trap with her hung in the air and his ego couldn't tolerate it another second. He gave her a benign smile. "Fine, let's go."

He winced when she slammed the door shut, but he scrambled out of the old truck and followed her. He was glad to see her checking the helicopter over before she opened the pilot's door. It creaked as badly as the old truck door, but he gritted his teeth and rounded the front of the chopper, struggling with the door handle before it finally jerked open and he was able to climb into the copilot's seat. He noted the frayed ends of the seat belt he snapped across his body, but it looked sturdy enough. He caught Tempe staring at his jeans.

"Something wrong?"

"Where'd you get those clothes?"

He looked down at himself. His jeans were properly starched—Dudley made sure of that—and he wore a plaid, Western-style shirt with pearl snap buttons. His cowboy boots were handmade and had cost five thousand dollars. There was nothing wrong with his attire.

"Dudley acquired proper clothing for me when I explained our destination."

Tempe shook her head and handed him a pair of earphones with an attached microphone as she began flipping switches. "You and your sidekick are a piece of work."

The whole contraption shook when the blades overhead started rotating. His seat vibrated and he gripped the torn armrest. "Are you sure this thing is safe?" he thought to ask just as the mini-beast lifted several feet off the ground.

Her answer was a thumbs-up and Ewen almost lost that wonderful breakfast as the thing rose. It rattled and shook until they were far enough into the air to die if it crashed, then the ride smoothed out a few minutes later and he was able to relax and enjoy the scenery.

From high up, he appreciated the flat, hardscrabble land that butted right up to a long line of foothills at the base of the majestic mountains, a major attraction of Big Bend National Park. It was beautiful, rugged terrain. He could only imagine the tough pioneers who'd tamed this land so many years ago. He itched to put pen to paper. He'd been thinking about changing his genre, and this place spiked his imagination. He glanced at Tempe, so confident in the pilot's seat, and a million questions filled his mind.

She pointed out the dingy window. "Our property goes right up to the base of the mountains."

He nodded and spotted the largest herd of beef cattle he'd ever seen. "How many?" he yelled into the microphone.

"We run over a thousand head of cattle."

He was impressed at the magnitude of the operation Tempe owned and operated and looked at her from a different perspective. Her dirty-blond hair was pulled back into a ponytail and she had on faded jeans. Her T-shirt had seen better days. Unlike his shiny new boots, hers were scuffed and worn. She didn't have on a stitch of makeup that he could detect, yet she was beautiful in a wholesome, tough kind of way. And she was handling the rattletrap they were flying in like a pro, which raised even more questions.

"Everything looks okay here. You wanna check

out our hot spring? It's a couple of miles west. We might even see Old Cyrus. He's a squatter who we allow to live near the hot spring. He pretty much stays to himself."

He nodded and his stomach rebelled when she banked the helicopter sharply to the left. A few minutes later, he spotted hills surrounding a small body of water. Intrigued, he leaned to his right and stared out the window just as he heard something that sounded like a rock hitting the plane. He jerked his alarmed gaze to Tempe. She morphed from a tough rancher into a warrior right in front of him, her expression grim and her alert gaze scanning the area below them from both the side and front windows.

"Is something wrong with the helicopter?" he asked and re-gripped the armrest of his seat.

Fire shot from her piercing green eyes when she turned toward him. "We have a problem."

A zillion things raced through his mind. Everything was in order. He'd updated his will six months ago, and his estate was in good hands, but he wasn't ready to die on a parched piece of land in the middle of nowhere. He sent up a quick prayer before asking, "What kind of problem?"

Those green eyes flashed anger instead of the fear he expected to see and for some reason that gave him a moment of comfort until she opened her mouth.

"Someone's shooting at us."

"What?" Yes, he'd been in the field many times during his tenure with the DIA, but for the most part he collected and analyzed intelligence on foreign militaries. He'd been shot at, but not while flying in a death trap. He didn't have a chance to say anything else because another volley of shots peppered the plane and Tempe gritted her teeth as she struggled to control the helicopter. He held on tight as she banked hard to the right, and back to the left.

Then he smelled the smoke, closed his eyes and truly experienced extreme fear for the first time in his life. He started praying as hard as he could, and soon a sense of peace settled over him. He didn't want to die, but if it was his time, he'd accept it. He opened his eyes and was startled, if not a little worried, when he looked at Tempe, seeing the light of battle in her eyes. Her words matched her expression.

"You think you can beat me, buster? Let's see who's the better woman," and after those ominous words, she started flying the chopper like a wild woman. Ewen had never seen anything like it. She banked a sharp right, then his shoulder hit the inside of the chopper when she cut it left so hard, the machine vibrated under the pressure. This went on for a minute or two, but after a fresh round of bullets hitting the machine, she glanced at him and yelled, "Hold tight, Scottie Boy, we're going down."

FIVE

As flashes from the crash she'd endured in her Hornet jet just over a month ago threatened to engulf her, Tempe's hands tightened on the yoke of the chopper, and through sheer will, she forced herself to calm down. She was a Blue Angel, a world-class pilot, and she could do this. Their lives depended on her keeping it together.

She'd been raised in the cockpit of various types of flying machines, and until the crash, she was the most confident pilot in her squadron. It irked her that this was happening, but like everything else in her life, she would overcome it.

The chopper pitched and rolled and her arms burned from fighting the out-of-control machine, but she refused to give in. She could do this, she reminded herself again. She had the best flight training the good ole US of A had to offer.

During one of the rolls, she caught sight of a jeep parked on top of a small hill and her heart almost stopped when a man standing beside the vehicle lifted what appeared to be an M3 sub-machine gun to his shoulder. If fired, the thing would obliterate the chopper. Someone meant to take them out. Permanently.

Her training kicked in and everything slowed in her mind, enabling her to focus. Instead of fighting the machine, she'd make it work for her. If the guy on the ground didn't take them out, they had a good chance of surviving this. She cut the engine, grasped the collective lever and soon had the blades under control. The rolling and pitching ceased and her irate passenger started yelling in his microphone.

"What happened? Did you just turn the engine off?"

For some reason, hearing Scottie Boy screech like a fishwife calmed her even more. One hand on the lever, she said, "Trust me, I know what I'm doing."

One glance at his face said that wasn't exactly what he wanted to hear, and she really did understand. She'd gained a job at his grandfather's castle under dubious circumstances, even if it was for a very good reason, and he didn't trust her. What she wasn't going to mention was the machine gun pointed straight at them. He'd really freak out if he had that small, but vital, piece of information.

To their right she spotted Old Cyrus throwing

himself on top of another rise and pointing a rifle in the direction of the jeep. The cavalry had arrived. He started shooting and the jeep soon disappeared, leaving a cloud of Texas dirt billowing behind it. One problem solved. Now all she had to do was get this pile of scrap metal safely on the ground.

She kept the blades spinning by maneuvering the collective lever, and slowly but surely the chopper began descending. It wasn't long before they touched down. It wasn't smooth, but they were in one piece.

She sat there a minute, savoring the fact that she'd done it. She'd flown since the crash, but this was the first time she'd faced a serious situation and her confidence soared. She had no doubts about flying with the Angels again, but it was good to know she could still handle the pressure. She'd been born to fly. It was in her blood.

A smile on her face, she unbuckled her seat belt and glanced at Ewen. He sat there, frozen stiff, his hands still gripping the worn armrests. She'd seen this before in pilots who didn't make the cut because they couldn't handle the pressure. Not wanting to startle him, she gently laid her hand over his.

"Hey, Scottie Boy, you okay?"

He dipped his chin and stared at her hand lying on top of his, as if that was somehow very significant. The thought made her uncomfortable and she tried to pull away, only to be stopped by his hand flipping over and grasping hers tightly.

His head lifted and the daze slowly faded from his eyes. "Aye, we're alive," he whispered, a deep Scottish brogue accenting his words.

She'd heard his brother, Ned, speak with a brogue when she was in Scotland, but not Ewen. She grinned at his unintentional slip into the accent he evidently tried so hard to keep hidden, and also because adrenaline still spiked through her system like rocket fuel. "Yeah, we made it."

He glanced at their intertwined hands as if he didn't know how that happened and jerked his away. The action pinged a sharp arrow near the region of her heart, but so what? He couldn't have made it more obvious that he wasn't attracted to her, and it wasn't important. She only wanted to get rid of him as soon as possible so she could get to save the ranch and finish her tour with the Blue Angels, didn't she?

Ignoring that silly question, she jerked open the pilot's door. "Let's make tracks before she decides to light up."

He gave her a blank look.

"In case the chopper catches fire. We've already got smoke coming out the back."

That snapped him back to reality and he scrambled out of the chopper as fast as his tall, lean muscular frame would allow. If the situation wasn't so serious, she might have laughed. As soon as she cleared the chopper, Old Cyrus greeted her from his usual distance—he didn't like people—with his ancient Springfield rifle still in his hand. The gun wouldn't have stopped the guy on the hill, but the intruder didn't know how many people were on the ground, and that was to their advantage.

"Looks like you got more trouble come your way."

Cyrus had been around for as long as she could remember, squatting on their property. Her granddaddy always said to leave him be, and today that had turned out to be a wise decision. No one knew much about him, but he kept to himself and never bothered anyone, so they left him alone. She'd very seldom seen him through the years. He was like the invisible man, most of the time.

Crossing her arms over her chest, she rocked back on her bootheels. "Yeah, and someone burned the barn down last night. You see anything unusual out this way?" Old Cyrus lived in a small cave in one of the foothills surrounding the hot spring.

"Nope, nuthin' going on around here I know of 'sides that man trying to shoot you out of the sky."

"I appreciate the help."

Old Cyrus nodded and glared at Ewen as he

approached. Ewen's straight, aristocratic brow arched as he glanced between the two of them. He pointedly shifted his gaze to the rifle in Old Cyrus's hand, but directed his comments to her.

"I assume he's not the one who shot at us or you wouldn't be having a peaceful conversation."

His clipped speech told her he'd gotten himself together after the almost crash, but she detected the strain beneath the veneer he presented.

"No, Cyrus didn't shoot at us. As a matter of fact, he saved our lives. I didn't want to mention it while we were in the air, but a guy parked on one of the small hills had a submachine gun pointed straight at us. Cyrus distracted him long enough for me to get the chopper landed."

Ewen's eyes narrowed and his voice became even more clipped. "You think someone tried to shoot us down? On purpose?"

"I don't think it, I know it."

Instead of commenting, he took a deep breath and held out a hand toward Old Cyrus. "It appears I have a lot to thank you for. Ewen Duncan. Pleased to make your acquaintance."

Tempe choked back a laugh when Cyrus looked at Ewen's hand, stared at his fancy cowboy duds, and turned back to her.

"Where'd ya find this fella? Don't look like he's from around here."

"Ewen, meet Cyrus. He lives here near the hot springs."

Ewen appeared baffled as he looked around for an abode of some sort, but Tempe intervened before he got Cyrus riled up with a bunch of questions. Even though she didn't see him often, something seemed off with Cyrus today.

"You okay, Cyrus? You seem a little different today."

"I'm okay."

The old man was definitely cleaner than usual. Maybe he'd decided to take a bath. It didn't matter; she had more important things to worry about. The sheriff would be arriving soon, and they needed to make tracks.

"Cyrus, we'll get this mess cleaned up as soon as possible," she said, pointing at the smoldering chopper. She glanced at Ewen's shiny new boots. "I hope those things are comfortable, 'cause we're gonna be hoofin' it back to the house."

Ewen stared at her. "I don't think so." He whipped out an unusual-looking smartphone and punched in a number. She was shocked when his valet answered and Ewen instructed him to bring the car. There were no phone towers anywhere close to their position.

With a smug expression, he said, "I own a satellite phone."

Huh! Maybe having the Scotsman hang around

for a while would be useful after all. If she could get him to stop hounding her about her time in Scotland, it would be even better.

Sliding into the cool interior of the limousine, Ewen ached to remove his boots. They were killing his feet. He ignored Dudley's questioning glance as the valet took in the smoking chopper and the ragged old man watching with sharp eyes as he stood there.

And that was another thing. Old Cyrus wasn't an old man. Ewen was a master at studying people, taking note of nuisances, and he knew without a doubt the wrinkles on Cyrus's face weren't real. They were expert enough to pass minimal scrutiny, but that was all. There was a reason Old Cyrus kept a safe distance from Tempe, and it had nothing to do with being a little strange.

Ewen briefly wondered how Dudley had managed to get the limo across the rugged territory, but the ground was flat and hard, which made a big difference. Pulling a bottle of water out of the mini-fridge, he broke the seal and took a good, long swallow. Ned had gone too far this time. Just because his brother was over-protective, military and ex-CIA—he had no idea Ewen was in the DIA—didn't give him the right to keep tabs on Ewen. He highly suspected Ned had stashed the real Cyrus somewhere else and placed one of his own men in his stead to keep an eye on his brother after Ewen had left Scotland in a hurry and without explanation to anyone and traveled to the middle of nowhere.

Lifting the water bottle to his mouth again, he stopped midair. What if Ned hadn't made the switch? What if the person trying to destroy Tempe's ranch had placed one of their own men there to cause trouble? Cyrus did shoot at the other fellow and got rid of him so they could land—if that could be called a landing—but maybe it was a ruse planned to throw them off track. The limo door stood open, waiting for Tempe to get in, and he watched her talking to the old man.

The guy could kill her where she stood and she wouldn't have a chance. Ewen was halfway out the limo door when she turned and took long strides toward him. With the sun at her back, her ponytail swished back and forth, and Ewen's heart stopped, all thoughts of murder and mayhem fleeing his mind.

She resembled a beautiful warrior woman. Strength and confidence flowed around her as she moved with smooth fluidity, and it hit him like a sledgehammer. He'd love to write a fictional novel based on this amazing woman.

He craved to know more about her—a woman who flew helicopters, got shot at, barely avoided a crash and walked away cool as a cucumber. He'd been searching for a new direction in his writing career and his gut was screaming this was it. If she gave her permission, and at this point, that was a big if.

It was nothing personal. The lady had lied to gain access to the castle, and she was an enigma. He would unravel every one of her secrets before it was over. But before he could do all that, he had to keep her safe. They had to discover the person responsible for trying to destroy her ranch, and that just might be connected to what she stole from the castle.

She slid into the seat beside him and closed the door as he scooted over. Dudley started the engine and they were on their way.

"I haven't thanked you for saving my life. That was an amazing landing. Where did you learn to fly?"

Her green eyes pierced him, then she shrugged. "You're welcome, and it's no big secret. I fly with the Blue Angels, but I'm on temporary leave."

He knew she'd been in the military, but he hadn't had time to find out what branch. He was highly impressed. "You're on leave because of what's happening at the ranch?"

She grunted and looked out the window of the limo. "Nosy, aren't you? I crashed my jet. I have a psych eval coming up. Soon, as a matter of fact."

This time he shrugged. "Nosiness goes with

the territory of being a writer." He leaned toward her. "Listen, Tempe, I'm good at what I do. I dig until I find the truth. I have contacts you can't imagine, and I can help you find out what's happening here. I can help you find the person responsible for trying to destroy your property, but you have to tell me everything because I need a starting point."

He held his breath. For some reason he wanted her to tell him the truth. When she didn't answer and just kept staring out the window, his inquisitive nature became active. But he waited patiently, something he was very adept at. Would she tell him why she lied to gain access to the castle?

She finally turned, suspicion filling her eyes. What did she have to be suspicious about? She was the big secret-keeper.

"What's in it for you? Why do you want to help a semi-stranger you don't trust?"

Because I want to prove you're not a traitor to your country by stealing or passing clandestine information to, and from, my grandfather's castle. The thought that sprang into his mind shook him. If it turned out she was working for an enemy of the US, he would turn her over to his superiors and she would be convicted. His stomach roiled at the thought.

He shrugged, trying to come up with an answer she would accept. "As I told you, I have international contacts, I know how to dig, and I want to help you and your daughter."

She raised a dirty-blond brow. "And why would I want someone rooting around in my business?"

Good point. He repeated his offer. "I can help you, Tempe."

She grinned and his heart thumped inside his chest.

"Okay, Scottie Boy, I'll think about it. You and your sidekick can spend another night and we'll see how it goes."

He didn't miss the glint in her eye. He knew she'd taken him up in that death trap to test his mettle and try and get rid of him. He prayed there wouldn't be any more tests of that nature. He wasn't ready to meet his Maker quite yet.

Ewen couldn't contain a grin when he spotted Kylo trying to herd what appeared to be the sheriff back to his car as Dudley pulled the limo in front of the house. He and Tempe exited the vehicle and after Tempe got control of the dog, the sheriff gave a long, low whistle as he stared at the big, black, dusty car.

"Well, well, well, what do we have here?"

Doc Hathaway hadn't fit Ewen's presumption of a small-town doctor, but the sheriff certainly matched the country lawman he'd been picturing. The man appeared to be in his early sixties. His hair was white and his girth definitely larger than the belt it protruded over, but there was something in the man's eyes that Ewen didn't like.

Ewen kept his mouth shut and let her handle the sheriff. She strode forward and held out a hand.

"I appreciate you coming out, John." They shook hands and she nodded at Ewen. "This is Ewen Duncan. Ewen, Sheriff John Brady. He's been around as long as I can remember."

Ewen shook the hand placed in front of him. "Nice to meet you, Sheriff." He could almost see the questions stirring in the sheriff's mind concerning Ewen's presence, but Tempe put a stop to that.

"Ewen is here on business."

Evidently there was some sort of unspoken code in the West about not butting into someone else's affairs, because the sheriff nodded and got to work at once. He pointed at the smoldering ashes where the barn used to be.

"Bart called last night, told me what happened. Anybody get hurt?"

"A few minor burns. Nothing serious. A man fled the scene at the barn and another one broke into the house, but they both got away. Arson is a definite possibility."

The sheriff tucked his thumbs into the waistband of his pants. "I asked around town. No one's seen anything out of the ordinary, but that doesn't mean someone couldn't be camped out in one of the old line-shacks the cowboys use on the trail."

Ewen addressed the sheriff. "Will you call in the fire department? They can discover how the fire started, maybe find a clue that would progress the investigation." The sheriff frowned but didn't respond, and Ewen pushed it a step further. "I have a lot of contacts. I can have an expert here tomorrow morning to sift through the rubble and find the point of origin and cause. If the fire was purposefully set—and I believe it was, based on the fleeing men—my people will discover it."

The sheriff frowned. "Now, see here, I don't know who you think you are, but out here we handle our own problems. We don't like outsiders poking into our business."

And that told Ewen everything he needed to know. The sheriff knew something the rest of them didn't, and Tempe was in big trouble.

Before Ewen could interrogate the sheriff further, a horse and rider came tearing into the driveway. Bart slid off the mare and bent over, catching his breath.

"Tempe, we got more trouble."

SIX

Tempe's anger overrode the icy tendrils of fear snaking around her neck, threatening to choke her. She'd had about enough. "What happened?" she snapped out.

Bart stood as straight as his bowed legs would allow and nodded at the sheriff before answering her. "We got fifty head of sick cattle in the south pasture. Looks to me like the pond's been poisoned."

Fury created a silent roar in her head, almost overpowering her ability to think straight. They couldn't afford to lose fifty head of cattle. They were teetering on bankruptcy as it was, but she unclenched her fists and silenced the chaos in her mind. She could handle this. She had no choice. And just where was this God whom Riley and Aunt Effie worshipped every Sunday? He certainly wasn't helping her save their home.

She answered Bart with a jerky nod. "I'll see to it," she said, then headed toward the horse corral. She heard Ewen question John, disbelief ringing in his voice.

"You're the sheriff. Aren't you going with her?"

"I have another emergency to see to and Tempe'll call if she needs me," John grumbled.

An excited Kylo on her heels, she headed for the old shack near the corral, thankful they'd stored the old, worn-out saddles there versus keeping them in the barn. Pulling the plank door open, she grabbed a saddle before turning and bumping into Ewen as she exited the building.

"I'm coming with you."

Tempe brushed past, but stopped and turned to face him. "Listen, this isn't your fight. Why don't you go back home before you get hurt? I won't be held responsible if something happens to a man of your stature." The last part came out rather snidely, but Tempe didn't care. She meant what she said.

He stiffened. "What do you mean by that?"

She was at the end of her rope and didn't care if she hurt his feelings. "Just what I said. You're rich, your family's rich and you're an internationally known author. I don't need more trouble."

Instead of getting mad and stomping off, he stood there, a thoughtful expression crossing his face. "A wealthy person hurt you in the past."

That hit too close to home and Tempe turned

away. "I don't care what you do. If you can manage to saddle a horse, you're welcome to join me," she said over her shoulder, but curiosity got the best of her when he only grinned and disappeared into the old shack.

She led her mare, Masie, out of the corral and watched curiously as Ewen reappeared toting an old Western saddle. He opened the corral gate and headed straight toward Bronco, a feisty stallion she planned to breed. "I'd advise you take the palomino. She's fairly placid."

He grinned again and expertly saddled the big horse. Tempe shrugged. He'd learn soon enough. She adjusted her saddle and mounted Masie in one fluid motion. She had to admit, Ewen appeared to know what he was doing, but she bit back a grin when he tried to mount Bronco. The stallion was barely saddle-broken and stood seventeen hands high. Bronco sidestepped, making it hard for Ewen to get a foot in the stirrup, but he finally made it atop the animal, albeit in an awkward manner.

Her humor fled and the anger returned when she turned Masie toward the south pasture. After a small struggle between man and horse, Ewen came up alongside her and they rode at a sedate but steady pace, Kylo running on the ground.

Ewen broke the silence, surprising her with a question. "Do you trust Sheriff Brady?"

She threw him a sharp glance. He resembled a Western magazine commercial, sitting atop Bronco with his pressed jeans, starched snap-button shirt and shiny new boots. The only nod to casual was the hair that brushed the collar of his shirt. But he did know how to dig for information, as evidenced by his bestselling novels. It might behoove her to find out what was stirring in that intricate brain of his before she sent him packing. "Why do you ask?"

He paused thoughtfully before answering. "I can't quite put my finger on it, but I don't trust the man. From what I understand, he hasn't done anything to help you find out who's trying to destroy your ranch."

That wasn't news. Tempe shrugged. "The Brewster County Sheriff's Department is headquartered in Alpine, two hours away from us. Brewster County is six thousand ninety-two square miles. Out here in the West, we tend to take care of things ourselves and call in the law when needed."

"You mean when you do his job, catch the perpetrators and call him in to pick them up?"

"You have city values, Scottie Boy. You don't know how things work out here."

He changed tack again and Tempe was impressed by his interrogation skills. "May I inquire about your military career?"

Even with her world falling apart, the man made her smile with his pretentious wording.

She gave him a speaking glance. "What you really want to know is about the crash, but I'll give you the background." She scanned the endless horizon, land that would still belong to her parents had they been alive.

"My dad was a Blue Angel and I was proud to follow his footsteps, but I didn't get into the program because of him. I joined the navy, worked my way up the ranks and became a commissioned officer. Lieutenant commander. I got on the flight team and proved myself in battle, after which I fiercely competed for a position in the Blue Angels. There's a term of two years in the unit and I've completed all but three months." She tightened her hands on the reins and Masie shifted uncomfortably, which forced Tempe to relax.

"And the crash?"

"Yeah, the crash. There was plenty of speculation in the news, but it's still under investigation as to the cause." Her stomach clenched because she knew with every fiber of her being that it wasn't human error. In her mind, she'd replayed every second of the crash, and she was 100 percent sure it wasn't her fault, even though plenty of people who didn't want women in the Blue Angels were fervently hoping that was the case.

"Didn't you say your parents were killed in a plane crash?"

His question startled her so much Masie shifted beneath her in reaction to Tempe's sudden stiffness. "What has that got to do with my crash?"

He shrugged, but the simple gesture didn't fool Tempe. Ewen had something on his mind and she wanted him to spit it out.

"Nothing in particular. Just gathering information."

"That happened eight years ago."

"Like I said, just gathering information. Was your father flying the plane when your parents died?"

Tempe stared straight ahead as the old anger reasserted itself. "Yes, but Dad was a brilliant pilot," she defended.

"Much like his daughter," he said, oh so casually.

"A wealthy person, or persons, hurt you." His subject changes had her head spinning. It wasn't a question, and Tempe almost told him to mind his own business because his insight into other people was unnerving, but why not answer his questions? Maybe he could see something she was missing.

She cleared her throat. "My mother's parents didn't approve of my father. They think their daughter married down. They're wealthy New

Yorkers and I met them for the first time at the funeral. They blamed my dad for my mother's death." She glared at him. "And that's all you're gonna get."

Goose bumps pricked Tempe's arms and she whipped her head around, scanning the foothills they'd almost reached.

"What is it?"

She continued to scan the area. "I'm not sure."

Tempe's sure-footed horse shifted nervously as dirt puffed the ground at Masie's feet. That was a bullet. "Go! Go! Go," she yelled at Ewen and Kylo, and took off for the protection of the closest foothill. She glanced over her shoulder just as Bronco reared up when another bullet hit the ground close to him. The stallion's eyes rolled, but Ewen held on. When the massive hooves hit the ground, the horse took off and there was no stopping him.

Ewen had ridden horses during the Scottish games at the castle, and he was arrogant enough to assume he could handle a stallion, and maybe even impress Tempe with his equestrian skills, but the horses he was used to had more training and were nothing like the feisty, heavily muscled beast beneath him. He was pretty sure someone was shooting at them and he had to get the horse under control, but, he thought morosely, at least the out-of-control animal made him less of a target.

He tried every tactic he'd been taught. He shortened the reins, braced one hand on the stallion's neck and grabbed his mane. That didn't work, so he pulled the reins toward his own shoulders, but the animal didn't respond.

He soon outpaced Tempe and her horse and flew past the small mound of hills that would have offered protection from the shooter. If he fell from the horse, he'd be trampled, so he hung on for dear life.

Out of the corner of his eye, he saw Tempe leaning over the neck of her horse, racing up on his left. When they were side by side, she reached out a hand and grabbed a fistful of Bronco's mane. Surely, she wasn't going to... Yes, she was.

She yelled into the wind, "I'm going to mount in front of you."

He shook his head in the negative, but before he could blink, she hoisted herself off her horse and onto his, right into the saddle in front of him. She snatched the reins out of his hands and he wrapped his arms around her waist. Within moments the horse started slowing down and finally came to a stop.

After Masie and Kylo caught up with them and Kylo barked once, they sat for a few seconds in silence, then Tempe slid off the horse and gazed up at him. She was breathing heavily but looked none the worse for wear. "You ready to go home now, Scottie Boy?"

Ewen just sat there on the horse, staring at this remarkable woman. She had to have been afraid, but she stood there boldly, reminding him of what her ancestors must have been like. Women who helped their men tame this wild land. A soft breeze lifted the dirty-blond ponytail off her shoulders, and she raised a proud chin. He'd never seen a woman more vibrant, brave or full of life.

He slowly dismounted and took a step toward her. He had the most disconcerting desire to kiss her, in the middle of this desolate territory, but reality slammed him like a fist in the chest when she took a step back and scrutinized him.

"You okay, Ewen?"

And just like that, he wanted to kiss her again, but he shook his head. What was wrong with him? Based on the video from the castle library, the woman could very well be a spy who'd stolen something from him. And he wasn't ready to trust any woman after some of the tricks that had been pulled on him in the past, in attempts to get him down the aisle. Plus, her life was a tangled mess. And she lived in Texas and he spent a good portion of his time in Scotland.

"I'm fine." For a man who was in the DIA and wrote books for a living, that was a pretty lame comment. He cleared his throat and tried once again. "It seems you saved my life. Again. Am I right in concluding that someone was shooting at us?"

She turned in a circle and scanned the area. "Yes, but we're safe now, too far away even for a sharpshooter."

"How can you be so calm? Someone is trying to kill or frighten you." He didn't give her time to answer. "Tempe, you need help."

She tilted her head and studied him for the longest time before answering. "I'm a highly trained officer and I fly. I perform well under extreme pressure."

"What about Riley and Aunt Effie? What if you're allowed to finish your last three months with the Blue Angels? Who is going to protect them?" He moved even closer. "Tell me the truth about what you were doing in Scotland and I'll help you. I'm very good at ferreting out corruption."

Both horses finally quit breathing heavily and settled down as he waited for her answer. He couldn't even explain to himself why this was so important, but he had that tingling feeling he always got right before things came together, whether it was a book he was writing or a case he was working on.

"You're welcome to stay here and risk your

neck, but I'm not answering any questions about my time at your grandfather's castle."

He released a breath he hadn't realized he'd been holding. He was in. He'd help Tempe find out who was trying to destroy her ranch and he'd get the answers he came for.

"You up for getting back on Bronco? I still need to check out the south pasture."

He eyed the horse warily before turning back to her, but refused to give her a reason to change her mind. "Of course, but don't you think you should call in some kind of authority besides Sheriff Brady? My brother, Ned, has a lot of contacts. You met him in Scotland. I can have someone out here tomorrow morning."

She shook her head and mounted her horse. "Maybe later, if we need them."

He gazed up at her, sitting so straight, tall and proud in her saddle. "You don't have to handle everything yourself." Another thought occurred to him. "Do you have faith, Tempe? Do you believe in God?"

A ripple of hurt shadowed her face. "Me and God haven't gotten along since Riley's no-good father left me pregnant when I was seventeen years old to raise a baby alone."

Well, that answered his question about Riley's father. "You can't blame God for that."

"Yeah? Well, I got pregnant not long after my

parents died. Life was hard and it felt like God was nowhere to be found."

She made a clicking noise with her mouth and lightly touched the reins on Masie's sides to get her moving. After promising Bronco a bucket of apples if he was allowed to mount, Ewen hopped aboard and followed Tempe to the south pasture.

She stopped above a small rise and he moved his horse beside hers. Nausea roiled in his stomach at the vista laid out in the valley before him. Scattered everywhere, beef cattle barely stood with their large heads hanging down in misery. A small pond sat in the middle. A lone rider came charging forward and stopped in front of them, Kylo barking and dancing around his horse. He had on worn jeans, a Western shirt and a huge cowboy hat. His boots were definitely worn in, unlike Ewen's new ones. He flicked a questioning glance at Ewen before addressing Tempe.

"Ma'am, they were fine yesterday when I checked on them. It had to have happened last night."

Remorse filled the cowboy's voice and Tempe cleared her throat before she spoke. This had to be hard on her. It was certainly hard on Ewen.

"It's not your fault, Tom. We'll have to be more vigilant. I know we're shorthanded, and I can't change that right now, but I'll take turns with you and the other men, watching the herds at night until we find out who's doing this."

Tom nodded. "I'll move them to a new pasture. Maybe fresh water will flush out the poison, if that's what made them sick."

Ewen prayed the animals would survive.

"I'll send some men to help you. We'll have to fence off the pond, make sure no other cattle stray into this area."

"I'll take care of it, boss," he said and turned his horse back down the slope.

Ewen had trouble taking it all in. How could someone do something this atrocious? And why?

"Tempe, does anyone have reason to want your land? Has someone approached you about buying your property?"

She sat there a moment and her hands tightened on the reins, then visibly loosened. Ewen watched her closely, studying her every movement and reaction.

Her lips curled into a sardonic, twisted smile. "Thomas Hildebrand tried to buy it from Granddad before he died because his property joins ours, and broached the subject again not too long ago with me, but I made it clear the land's not for sale."

"Could he want your land badly enough to get rid of you, ensuring your ranch is sold?"

SEVEN

Tempe turned away from the sick cattle, feeling a little sick herself and pointed Masie toward home. For the first time in her life, she was at her wits' end. Everything was spinning out of control. Her checking account was dwindling, and she'd banked on the yearly cattle sale to help them make it through the end of the year. Hopefully, the cattle would survive, but it would hurt if they didn't. Her military salary helped, but she'd already decided to muster out after she completed her stint with the Blue Angels. Riley needed her mom at home.

She considered all the questions Ewen had asked earlier when he said he was gathering information. Were any of the previous events in her life related to what was happening at the ranch now? She couldn't make a connection. She glanced at Ewen, and a small part of her was glad he was around. She hated to admit it, but she needed some help. Maybe he was right, maybe it was time to call in an expert to help her figure out what was going on.

"Have you called the insurance company about the barn?"

His question broke the silence and pulled her out of her reverie. "There is no insurance."

She glanced at him when he didn't respond. "As a keen man of observation, I'm sure you've noticed there are repairs needed around the ranch. Money's been tight for a couple of years due to a drop in cattle futures." She didn't mean to sound disgusted, but that was how she felt. Time to veer the subject away from her financial problems. "Who would you call?"

"What?"

"Who would you call to help me find out who's destroying my ranch?" She glared at his surprised expression. "I handle most things around here, but I know when I need help, and you're right, the sheriff hasn't done much of anything about the situation." She sent him a sharp glance. "I can't afford to pay much."

His lips curved upward. "If you could bring yourself to look past that pride you wear like armor, you might find some people are willing to help simply to see justice done." He went on before she could snarl a response to that bit of nonsense. "I spoke of Ned earlier. You met him at his wedding in Scotland."

She nodded, knowing he was itching to ask again why she'd been at the castle, but he held his tongue.

"He's ex-CIA and has a lot of contacts. I have a few myself from my writing career, but his people are better trained for this type of situation."

She didn't like it, but she had no choice. "Fine, call him and see what he says, but don't give him the green light on anything until you talk to me."

He agreed and Tempe soon caught sight of the house, but groaned out loud when she spotted the Range Rover parked in the driveway. Kylo was barking his head off.

"What is it?" he asked, tension filling his voice.

Tempe grinned. "Don't worry, we're not getting shot at again. That vehicle in the driveway belongs to Thomas."

He glanced at her sharply. "Thomas Hildebrand? The man who wants to buy your property?"

His eyes burned with curiosity and she was coming to recognize that look. He'd had the same expression when asking about her parents' deaths and her plane crash.

"Is he married?"

"Yes. Why?"

He raised a brow. "It's a simple question."

She shook her head. "Not with you, it's not. I agree with the media when they say you have a Machiavellian mind. I can see that brain of yours coming up with all kinds of plots and twists. Just remember this is real life."

"All this because I asked about his marital status?"

"No, because you're trying to link Thomas Hildebrand to the destruction on my ranch and there's no way it could be him. He married money and has no reason to do any of this."

"Didn't you say he offered to buy your ranch before your grandfather died?"

"Yes, but they were good friends."

Tempe guided Masie to the corral and Ewen followed her. Kylo made a beeline toward the house. Just as she pulled the saddle off her horse, Thomas came running up, all puffed up with his own consequence. He totally ignored Ewen as he took the saddle from her and hung it on the fence.

"Tempe, you should have called me. I was at the café when I heard about the barn. Is everyone okay?"

After her conversation with Ewen, she couldn't help scrutinizing Thomas more closely. He was shorter than Ewen but still considered tall at six feet. His neatly trimmed dark hair showed signs of silver at the temples. He had on jeans and a Western shirt, not as neat as Ewen's, but his clothes hung on his frame well. He looked like the perfect candidate for governor. Did he want her property badly enough to cause the destruction? She shook her head. They'd been neighbors forever, helped each other out from time to time, and her grandfather had trusted him. She refused to believe he was responsible for her recent problems.

"We're fine. You didn't need to drive all the way out here to check on us. I'm sure you have enough on your plate, with the election coming up."

Thomas's eyes narrowed when Ewen stepped forward and held out a hand, all affable, but Tempe knew better. Her temporary guest had interrogation in mind.

"Ewen Duncan."

"Thomas Hildebrand," Thomas responded. But he directed his next question to Tempe. "A friend of yours?"

Tempe had had enough. She wanted Thomas gone. She had a lot to take care of. She shot Ewen a warning glance to keep his mouth shut. "Yes, and I appreciate you coming by, Thomas," she said as she steered him toward his car, "but I have work to do."

Ewen kept pace with them and Tempe wanted to muzzle him when he opened his mouth.

"Not only did the barn burn down, but someone tried to shoot down Tempe's helicopter. They also took shots at us on horseback while we were riding to the south pasture where we're pretty sure someone poisoned fifty head of her cattle."

Thomas suddenly pivoted and grabbed Tempe's shoulders with both hands. "Tempe, is this true? You could have been killed." He stepped back and Tempe noticed his face had gone pale. She might not care all that much for the man, but he wasn't the culprit in all of this.

She gentled her tone. "I'm fine, and we'll find out who's doing this and put a stop to it. I appreciate your concern."

"What about Riley and Effie? Are they safe here?"

The accusation in his tone had Tempe stiffening. "Of course, they're safe. I can take care of my own."

His face softened, but it did nothing to soothe Tempe's ire.

"I'm sorry. I didn't mean to imply otherwise. You're a courageous woman."

Ewen stepped into the fray and Tempe wanted to strangle him.

"No worries. I'm here to help as long as Tempe needs me."

Thomas whirled around. "Just who are you?"

Ewen rocked back on the heels of his shiny new boots. He winked at Tempe, and Thomas's nostrils flared.

"I'm a friend. A good friend."

Time to intervene. She could blast Ewen for nosing into her business after she got rid of Thomas. "I appreciate you stopping by, Thomas."

He gave her a gentle smile. "Please let me know if I can do anything to help."

Tempe waited until he got into his car and left, before turning her wrath on Ewen. "I have agreed to let you stay and help, but I have to maintain a good relationship with Thomas because his property joins mine. Sometimes cattle escapes onto other people's property, and it's nice if there's not a feud going on."

Ewen frowned. "I don't like him. Just tell me this, Tempe, how did your grandfather die?"

Leaving his question hanging in the air, Tempe pivoted on her heel and headed toward the house. As Ewen swept inside the house behind her, he could see that pandemonium reigned.

Ewen's valet had a full apron tied around his body with the saying Kiss the Cook blazoned across the front. He held a dripping spoon in his right hand, a look of horror stamped on his face. Aunt Effie had some sort of batter splashed across her face and clumps of the same matter in her hair. Riley was bent over at the foot of the stairs in the foyer, squealing with laughter, but the real culprits, Kylo and Simba, were cowering in the corner, safeguarding a stack of pancakes scattered within close proximity.

He wondered how the dog had managed to get inside the house and create so much havoc so quickly.

Taking in the scene, Tempe placed two fingers in her mouth and released a whistle piercing enough to bust an eardrum. Everyone in the room stopped, frozen in position with comical expressions on their faces.

He and Tempe glanced at each other and he saw her mouth twitch, then blossom into a full-blown grin. That wide grin made his heart thump against his chest so hard he was afraid everyone would hear it. She winked at him before putting a mock-stern look on her face and addressing the rambunctious group.

"Kylo, you know better," she addressed her dog.

The once-proud Australian shepherd hung his head in shame. The big fat tabby cat lifted his nose at everyone and proceeded to groom himself, as if he hadn't created a maelstrom. Ewen had no doubt that Simba had been the instigator.

He shot Dudley a hard look and his valet cleared his throat. "Yes, well, I think we'll just get this mess cleaned up."

Effie smiled at Dudley and nodded. "I'll help you." She turned toward Tempe. "And you, young lady, can fill me in on today's happenings after dinner. I saw Thomas Hildebrand and the sheriff's cars in the drive."

Tempe nodded. "Yes, ma'am. Pancakes for dinner?"

A wide smile spread across Effie's face and Ewen realized she really was a lovely woman.

"Riley requested them. Now go upstairs and clean up. Supper'll be ready in thirty minutes and you missed lunch."

Tempe disappeared up the stairs and Ewen stood there for a second until Effie raised a brow at him. He got the message and turned to climb the stairs. Once in his room, he removed a sleek laptop from a hidden compartment in his luggage. Even if Tempe had Wi-Fi, he wouldn't use any communication so easily hacked into. A lot of his calls and correspondence were classified, but he'd even gone so far as to write a program for his personal computer that blocked the DIA from scrutinizing his personal email or phone calls, because they were a nosy bunch. His business with Tempe had nothing to do with his position at the DIA, or so he hoped, so he clicked his firewall program, set up a satellite relay and connected his laptop—one he'd changed to meet his criteria.

His brother, Ned, was extremely computer savvy, but his skills were nothing compared to

Ewen's. None of his family, including Ned, knew of his position with the DIA, because most of his work was done on his computer. They assumed all of his work time was spent writing novels.

His valet, Dudley, was the only person who knew the truth, and Ewen trusted him implicitly. Ewen's position at the DIA mainly comprised collecting and analyzing intelligence on foreign militaries. The DIA's mission statement was to "prevent and decisively win wars." Which meant he rarely traveled to DIA headquarters in Washington, DC. As far as field agents were concerned, Ned had better connections. The phone rang once and Ewen heard the satisfying click that told him the line was secure.

Ned growled on the third ring. "This better be important."

"It is."

"Ewen, is that you? Why didn't you say so?"

Ewen smiled. The two brothers were very close. Maybe it was time to share his secret life with Ned. He should have done it sooner, but the family really worried about Ned when he was in the CIA, and everyone was relieved when he quit the job. Ned had always been so protective over everyone in the family, Ewen had chosen to keep the information to himself. But Ned always intruded into Ewen's business anyway.

"I just did."

A gruff chuckle filtered through the line. "What's up?"

Ewen grinned. So his brother wanted to play dumb? "You ever hear the name Old Cyrus?"

There was a telltale millisecond of hesitation that Ewen didn't miss, so he plowed on without giving Ned a chance to speak. "Which watchdog did you send to keep an eye on me and where is the real Old Cyrus?"

A heavy exhale, then, "Busted. I worry about you. It's not a crime. You're my brother and I don't see a problem."

Ewen decided to cut him some slack. Ned had no way of knowing that Ewen could help start or stop World War III with the sensitive information he filtered through on a daily basis.

"Who's living in a cave on Tempe Calloway's ranch?"

"Simon."

Ewen sighed. "Where is Old Cyrus?"

Ned chuckled again. Married life really agreed with his surly brother. "He's living the good life for a couple weeks off the California coast."

"And what prompted you to send Simon to keep an eye on me? Simon must have gotten here before I did."

"Alfred contacted me when you took off after

the librarian Grandfather hired. I viewed the same surveillance tape that you did. This Maggie Sutherland, or rather, Tempe Calloway is up to no good."

Ewen pinched the bridge of his nose. "Our castle butler is much too nosy." It made Ewen wonder what else the wily old man knew.

"Well, it's a good thing I sent Simon. He reported you were almost shot down in a helicopter. Sounds to me like he saved your life."

Ned had him there. "I do appreciate that, but Ned, I can take care of myself. You need to stop trying to rescue me every time a little trouble comes my way. I write novels for a living. How dangerous could my life be?"

Silence. "Ned?"

"When you get home, you and I need to have a talk."

Had Ned somehow found out about his primary career? Maybe so, but now wasn't the time. He had to help Tempe, and at the same time, find out what she'd stolen from the castle library.

"Let me catch you up to speed." Ewen filled him in on everything that had happened at the ranch. Ned listened quietly, then grumped, "You sure know how to pick 'em, Ewen."

Ewen stiffened. "I didn't pick Tempe Calloway for anything other than trying to find out why she was in Scotland."

"Tell me what you need."

"I'd like a few men to join Simon, if that's possible, just in case things escalate."

"What else?"

Ewen could run a search on the men himself, but with everything going on, he could use the help. "I'd like to know everything you can find on a man named Thomas Hildebrand. He tried to buy Tempe's ranch a long time ago, and then again more recently. Tempe doesn't think he'd commit criminal acts just to buy the land that borders his, but I don't trust the man. And if you could check one other person, I'd appreciate it. Sheriff John Brady. There's a possibility he could be the one implementing them."

"You got it, brother. Anything else?"

Ewen cleared his throat. "We'll definitely talk when I get home." Before things got too sappy, he popped in one last question. "How did Simon get here before I did?"

Ned laughed gruffly. "I'm ex-CIA. You figure it out," he replied, then the line went dead.

Ewen waited for the telltale click before disconnecting the call. He turned off the program and cleared the history, so if anyone went looking, they'd never discover usage on the satellite or his laptop.

Slipping the computer back inside the disguised suitcase compartment, he cleaned himself up and, with a surprising spring in his step, went to gorge himself on pancakes.

EIGHT

The next morning, with a booted foot propped on the bottom rail of the corral fence, Tempe felt more than heard Ewen quietly come up beside her.

"What's going on? What are the barrels for?"

Numerous times, she'd asked herself why she was allowing him and his valet to stay at the ranch, but deep down she knew. He had offered to help discover who was trying to destroy her ranch, and it felt good to share some of her burdens versus going it alone. And she unwisely found herself attracted to the man, but since that was never going anywhere, she ignored it. Now wasn't the time for introspection. She wanted to see her daughter enjoy herself for a change. Riley carried too much on her young shoulders and it was time for her daughter to have some fun.

She lifted the timer in her hand. "You're about to find out. Go!" she yelled.

Riley and Buckeye came barreling through the

open gate and Tempe grinned when Ewen stiffened beside her. She watched as her daughter raced toward the first barrel, pride swelling in her chest at this wonderful child she was so fortunate to call her own. Riley's long, dirty-blond hair whipped behind her from beneath the brown cowboy hat, and a stripe down the side of her jeans matched the dark pink Western shirt covered in sewn-on patches from previous wins.

Riley handled Buckeye with confidence and ease, she and the horse moving in perfect harmony. She'd worked so hard to get to the Dixie National Super Show, and no matter what happened with the ranch, Tempe would do whatever it took to make sure she was able to compete.

By the time Riley rounded the second barrel, Ewen was white-knuckling the top fence rail. Before they reached the third barrel, Tempe dropped her foot to the ground and tensed. Something was wrong. Her gaze moved from the unnatural shift Riley made in the saddle to the horse's eyes, which were so wild the whites were showing.

Tempe automatically jumped the railing and started running toward Riley and Buckeye, but before she could reach them, the horse screamed, reared up and pawed the air. Being an expert rider, Riley hung on, but Tempe's heart lodged in her throat when she saw that Riley was going to make an elective jump off the horse versus trying to control the situation. When Buckeye reared a second time, it felt like everything happened in slow motion.

Tempe was only a few strides away when Riley released the reins and allowed herself to slide off the back of the animal. She hit the ground and rolled to the side, just as she was taught in this type of situation. Giving Riley time to get out of the way, Tempe approached Buckeye, garnering his attention. His sides were heaving, gasping for air, but the wild look in his eyes had calmed a bit. Tempe breathed a sigh of relief when Riley scrambled to her feet and calmly walked toward them. Her daughter was okay.

With a soothing tone, Tempe slowly approached the horse. "It's okay, Buckeye. Did something spook you, boy?" Slowly lifting her hand, she grabbed the reins and gently laid a hand on the side of his head. "It's okay."

Riley came up beside her. "Whatever happened isn't his fault, Mama. Halfway through the run, I felt him tense. I knew something was wrong and that I should get off instead of trying to control him."

Tempe nodded. Riley had been on a horse since she could walk, and she had good instincts. "Let's take the saddle off and give him a good rub down while we figure out what happened."

Tempe's words came out calm, confident and

strong, but her mind was whirling with what-ifs. What if Riley had gotten injured, or worse? If anything had happened, Tempe would never have forgiven herself.

They walked Buckeye around the ring several times to cool him down, but he was still jittery. Tempe gently unhooked the girth strap, grabbed both ends of the saddle and slowly pulled it to the side and off Buckeye, then she removed the saddle pad and gasped. Blood was spurting from a wound in the middle of his back, right where Riley's weight would be—creating the maximum amount of damage.

She took a deep breath before turning the saddle upside down on the ground and inspecting the leather, wanting to be sure of her suspicions. Unfortunately, they were confirmed as she smoothed a hand over the underside of the leather and felt something.

She flipped the saddle back over and dug out a sharp tack with her fingers. Standing, she stared at the bloody culprit. Someone had sabotaged her daughter's saddle. Tempe started shaking and she couldn't seem to stop. Riley could have been killed!

Fury mixed with fear—a lethal cocktail—made her shake even more. Riley stood to the side, quietly talking to Buckeye, calming him even further, but she had tears in her precious eyes when she looked up at Tempe.

"Mama, I checked everything twice. This is my fault," Riley said, glancing at the wound on Buckeye's back. Her lips trembled and Tempe snapped out of her own emotional state, kneeled in front of her daughter and placed her hands on the little girl's shoulders.

"Riley, listen to me. This isn't your fault. I'm pretty sure whoever has been trying to destroy the ranch did this as a warning to me."

Riley lifted her smooth-as-cream face. "But Mama, we still don't know who's doing it and why."

Tempe wrapped Riley in her arms, so relieved her daughter was safe that it nearly stole her breath. Pulling back, she forced a smile. "Why don't you go grab the first aid kit and we'll take care of Buckeye." She held up the tack and studied it. "The wound can't be very deep, based on the size of this tack. He should be okay in a week or so, time enough to compete in the Dixie Classic three weeks from now."

Riley swiped her eyes with the sleeve of her shirt and nodded. "I'll be back in a few minutes."

Tempe knew Ewen, who had climbed over the fence earlier, had overheard their conversation. She appreciated that he waited on the sidelines and let her handle Riley without interfering. He moved closer and glanced pointedly at the tack in her hand. Tempe had started shaking again, this time in fury.

"Whoever's been trying to destroy my ranch just crossed the line. They can come after me, but nobody makes a move against my daughter and gets away with it. Nobody!"

Ewen didn't say a word. He didn't try to tell her what to do. When he did finally speak, it was music to her ears.

"How can I help?"

Her heart thumped hard in her chest. Unlike most men, he didn't try to tell her everything would be okay, and then run over her trying to take over. He simply stood there and waited.

She looked into those bold blue eyes of his and took a breath as the wind brushed his rich, reddish-brown hair against his collar. She felt a connection unlike anything she'd ever felt with a man, but she immediately shook it off. She would never trust anyone with her heart again. It was too painful. Pushing aside that depressing thought, she tightened her fists and gave a jerky nod.

"You said you wanted to help."

He nodded. "Anything you need."

Tempe didn't like owing anyone, but the ugliness had touched her daughter, and she would do anything to stop this madness. She jerked when he touched her chin and gently lifted her head.

"I already have a few things in the works I need to tell you ab—"

"Well," a snippy voice intruded, "I see we arrived just in time."

Tempe snapped her head toward the woman she'd never expected to see again.

"The information we received seems to be correct," the woman dressed to the nines said. She sniffed and lifted her patrician nose in the air. "We're here to gain custody of our great-granddaughter."

Anger rocketed through Ewen on behalf of Tempe and Riley. He ignored the fact that he himself had been terrified to see such a young person astride a large, fast horse a few moments earlier. Not much shocked him due to his choice of careers, but when he turned and spotted Minerva Roderick and her husband, Franklin, standing outside the corral fence, threatening to take Tempe's daughter away from her, he was definitely surprised. Even more astonishing was discovering they were Tempe's grandparents. She'd mentioned them but never told him their names.

Based on the thunderous expression building on Tempe's face, he knew he had to do something, so he subdued his own anger, stepped forward and extended a hand over the railing. Time to pull out the big guns of sophistication, which he knew entailed the language Minerva would understand.

"Ewen Duncan. I believe you know my grandfather."

He could see the woman processing his name at warp speed, and knew the moment she realized who stood in front of her. Her expression underwent a drastic change, even though her smile was tight.

"You're Angus Duncan's grandson. The writer."

Ewen inclined his head. He knew exactly how to handle these people. He'd been exposed to enough of them through his family's art business, and because of his grandfather's status in the world as laird of a castle in Scotland. He'd seen the Rodericks at a few functions but was never inclined to meet them personally.

Minerva seemed at a loss for words, which Ewen doubted happened often, but she did manage to get in a dig at Tempe.

"I can't imagine what someone of your stature is doing at a remote ranch in Texas."

Ewen turned to include Tempe in the conversation, but realized she was bent over, having a whispered conversation with Riley. Of course, Riley would be her first concern. Tempe might be tough, and her daughter was being raised differently than most kids her age, but Ewen had no doubt Tempe would give her life for her daughter. He switched his gaze to Riley and curiosity, anger and a touch of fear was stamped on her young face. That created another surge of outrage at the manner in which the Rodericks were handling this situation.

Ewen stepped back when Riley left her mother's side and boldly walked up to the railing, stopping in front of the great-grandparents he assumed she'd never met.

"You're my great-grandparents?" Her question proved his assumptions correct, and he marveled at the maturity of the eight-year-old.

Minerva's face softened a bit—the first maternal sign she'd given so far. Ewen's heartstrings hummed at the sight being played out in front of him and a ton of questions filled his mind. The Rodericks were filthy rich. Had they offered to help Tempe and her sister after their parents died?

For just a moment, Minerva actually looked like she wanted to climb over the fence separating her from her great-granddaughter. Instead she stepped closer to the wood railing in a dignified manner.

"Yes, darling, we're your grandmother's parents. We live in New York in a fabulous penthouse overlooking the park. We'd like for you to come live with us because we've been informed dangerous things have been happening here at the ranch."

Ewen wondered just who had informed them. He looked back at Tempe and saw something unexpected. For the first time since he'd met her, she appeared defeated, but the expression disappeared. She straightened her shoulders and moved beside Riley.

Ewen decided another intervention was called for before Tempe pulled out some sort of weapon and ran her grandparents off the property. This would have to be handled properly. There was no way the grandparents would ever win custody in court, but he also knew Tempe didn't have the money to fight them, and that might pose a real problem.

"Riley, it's hot out here. Why don't you and Kylo take your great-grandparents inside? Tempe and I will make sure Buckeye is taken care of, then we'll join you."

Tempe looked as if she wanted to grab her daughter and disappear, but gave a jerky nod of agreement. As soon as Riley and the Rodericks disappeared from view, she vented her wrath.

"I can't believe after all these years they showed up like that, threatening to steal my daughter. They threw away their own daughter, and if they expect to take mine, they have another think coming."

Tempe's face was flushed and her hands were fisted at her sides. She reminded him of both a warrior and a mother bear protecting her young. Her eyes were lit, ready for battle.

Ewen tamped down his anger on her behalf and placed both hands on her shoulders. He felt tremors racking her body. "Tempe. Listen to me. I know you're upset, but you have to calm down. We have to handle this properly."

She spoke through gritted teeth, "They. Will. Not. Take. Riley!"

He needed to pacify her and get some answers before they went inside. While they were talking, Bart had moved Buckeye to the other side of the corral and was taking care of his wound, so they didn't have to worry about the horse.

Ewen gazed into her eyes. His heart gave another lurch when he saw the tears pooled in their green depths. He had to remind himself that he didn't fully trust this woman, but that was a different issue. He had no doubt Tempe loved her daughter.

"Listen, just listen to me for a moment," he repeated when she stepped away from him and his arms fell to his sides.

"Minerva and Franklin Roderick will never gain custody of your daughter. We'll make sure of that."

"We?" she asked, sarcasm lacing her words.

"Who's this *we*? I asked for help finding out who is trying to destroy my ranch. This is a personal matter, and I'll handle it myself."

Ewen searched for the right words because he wanted to help Tempe and Riley. He might not trust the woman, but he refused to stand by and see her lose her daughter, even if he didn't think a judge would ever give custody to the great-grandparents.

"Tempe, we need to find out who informed the Rodericks about happenings here at the ranch. That information might lead to the person, or persons, trying to destroy you and your ranch."

She looked stunned for a moment, then whispered, "Do you think someone hates me enough to have my daughter taken from me?"

His gut screamed that it was all connected, and he was a master at analyzing information and coming to conclusions. In his line of work, it sometimes started or stopped a war.

"I don't think *hate* is the correct word. Someone wants you or your property destroyed for a reason, and we're going to find out why."

He waited a beat, then said, "Tempe, I need information to form conclusions. Tell me about your grandparents and why they obviously haven't been in your life."

He listened as she quietly told an all-too-familiar story of a wealthy family who didn't approve of the man their daughter wanted to marry and cut all ties and money. With a soft smile, Tempe stressed that her mother more than willingly gave up everything because she was so in love with Tempe's father, but she always regretted having to make a choice.

"Did your mother ever try and contact her parents?" Ewen asked.

Tempe nodded. "Every so often she'd write them a letter, but it was always returned, unopened."

"Did they come to your parents' funeral?"

Tempe dipped her chin. "That's the first time I met them, and they didn't acknowledge any of us. They came for the funeral and immediately left. Other than that, I never heard a word from them until today. Of course, I didn't have Riley then. Maybe discovering they have a great-granddaughter changed things."

He gazed into those troubled and angry eyes. "Tempe, this is your family, and you'll handle it the way you think best. I'm only suggesting you take your time and gather as much information as possible, and who knows, maybe they've had a change of heart and this gave them an opportunity to save face."

Before she could respond, a loud boom shook the ground beneath their feet. They both jerked their heads toward the house and saw flames racing toward the front porch roof.

"Riley," Tempe whispered, and started running toward the house with Ewen close on her heels.

NINE

If God hadn't abandoned her, Tempe would be praying right about now. Instead, she headed straight for the water hose Aunt Effie used to take care of the flowers in front of the house, hating that her hand shook as she turned on the spigot.

Ewen came up behind her and picked up the hose, pointing it toward the flames. "Go around back and make sure everyone got out. I'll take care of the fire. It's not quite as bad as it sounded."

His surety and command of the situation eased her mind and assuaged her fears a bit, but she still hesitated a split second before taking off around the side of the house. She heard Kylo's excited barking before she rounded the corner and breathed a sigh of relief when she spotted everyone outside, with Kylo staying close to Riley and Riley trying to calm down her great-grandmother.

Dudley appeared to be trying to comfort Aunt Effie, but Tempe's aunt was made of sterner stuff and pushed away the arm he tried to place around her shoulder. Tempe released the breath she was holding. Everyone was okay, and that was the most important thing—at least it was until Minerva Roderick broke away from Riley and approached Tempe in a fit of righteous fury. Franklin stood to the side, his arms crossed over his chest.

Her hair hadn't moved an inch due to the massive amount of hair spray, but otherwise the woman was slightly disheveled, which Tempe doubted happened often.

The woman pointed a trembling finger at Tempe. "This is why we're taking Riley. It's too dangerous for her to stay here. First this fire, and then that beast—" she pointed at Kylo "—bit me on the rump. I'll not allow my great-granddaughter to stay here another moment."

Tempe took a deep breath, keeping in mind what Ewen said about collecting information and getting answers, but before she could speak, Riley moved to her great-grandmother's side and touched her vein-littered, ring-adorned hand. "Great-Gamy, that's Kylo's job, to herd things, and he's still young and in training. He was only trying to herd you out of the house so you wouldn't get hurt. He didn't bite you, he tried to save your life."

Before Minerva could respond, Simba came

sauntering out the back door like a king and wrapped himself around Minerva's legs. She looked down, an expression of horror crossing her face.

"Get that cat away from me. I'm allergic to the creatures."

This was serious business and Tempe took control of the situation. "Minerva—" she couldn't stomach calling her Grandmother "—first of all, Riley isn't going anywhere." She scanned the area, looking for more threats. The fire was probably started with a timer and the perpetrator long gone, but there was no need to take chances.

Ewen came up beside her. "Bart is taking care of the rest of the fire. I checked the house. It's safe to go back in. The fire is contained, soon to be extinguished."

Tempe nodded and turned back to Minerva and Franklin. "We need to take this inside. We're sitting ducks out here."

Tempe felt a moment of pity when the older woman turned a pasty shade of white after the meaning of her words sank in, but they needed to move. She called Kylo off when he trotted around to the back of the group, ready to do his job. The last thing they needed was another herding "nip."

Minerva pivoted sharply on her expensive heels and entered the side door leading to the kitchen, her docile husband scurrying close behind. When they all got inside, Tempe motioned everyone toward the scarred oak table, refusing to be embarrassed about the worn look of the place. Her grandparents were there threatening to take her daughter away, and she wasn't feeling particularly social. She pulled Riley to her side and gave her a hug.

"Why don't you take Kylo and Simba upstairs? We adults need to have a talk."

Tempe's stomach clenched when Riley got the stubborn expression on her face that Tempe knew so well.

"No, Mama. Y'all are going to talk about me and I have a right to hear what's going on." Riley speared a look at her great-gamy—Tempe briefly wondered what her upper-crust grandmother thought of that nickname—then added a sweet smile before saying, "And Great-Gamy, I really would like to get to know you since my other grand and great-grandparents are dead, but I might as well tell you now, I'm not leaving my Mama. She needs me.

"I have an idea." Riley turned pleading eyes on Tempe, but kept speaking to her great-grandparents. "You can stay here for a while. That way we can visit and you can see that me and Mama can take care of ourselves."

Tempe's stomach churned. She didn't want Minerva and Franklin here, and she didn't want to give her grandparents any additional ammunition to use against her in a custody battle, but fear of the situation was reflected in Riley's eyes, plus something else. Was that eagerness to get to know her great-grandparents Tempe was seeing? Riley knew the story of what happened to Tempe's mother all those years ago, but she'd never said anything about contacting her great-grandparents. Had Riley stayed quiet because she knew Tempe didn't care for Minerva and Franklin?

Surprising everyone, Minerva sniffed and raised her chin. "That will be acceptable, but I have a few rules. The dog and cat stay outside."

Well, now, Tempe thought, Ewen claimed to know how to handle "these" kind of people, so Tempe decided to let him have at it. "Ewen, why don't you, Effie and Dudley see to getting everyone settled, and I'll go outside and check, see what Bart's come up with as to the cause of the fire."

Minerva looked like she wanted to spew forth some words, but Tempe shot her a don't-mess-with-me look and the woman's mouth formed a thin line. That was more like it. They had a serious situation and Tempe didn't need more problems. She whistled and Kylo bounded past everyone in the room and followed her out the side door. As soon as she was out of sight, she leaned against the side of the house and closed her eyes.

She had always been able to handle most anything, but things were stacking up, and something had to be done. As much as she hated to admit it, Minerva was right. Riley was in danger—they all were—and it was Tempe's job, as head of the household, to make sure everyone was safe. This was almost as bad as when her parents died. At only seventeen years old, she'd had to grow up fast. On the heels of that, she'd found herself pregnant.

She stayed where she was when Ewen joined her outside. He leaned against the house beside her.

"Tempe, you're not alone in this. I told you I'd help, and I mean that."

She barked out a laugh and shook her head. "If you want to help, keep my grandparents as far away from me as possible. I can't believe after all this time they're now staying in my house. I don't need this complication."

He took her hand, and startled, she lifted her head. "As I was trying to tell you before the fire, I contacted Ned for help. It appears he thought I would need some assistance, because Old Cyrus is having the time of his life somewhere on the California coast. Ned already has one man in place disguised as Old Cyrus, and more men are on the way."

"Why'd he do that?"

Ewen shook his head and sighed. "Ned thinks I can't take care of myself. After I left, he reviewed the same castle library tape I did—the one that showed you removing something from a book and slipping it into your pocket. You disappeared after that. He knew I was on my way here and decided I might need help. He had Simon in Old Cyrus's place before I arrived."

"I don't have a lot of extra money," Tempe said bluntly, but she sure did need the help.

"Tempe, Ned has already hired Simon to be my watchdog, so he's protecting me as much as anyone. Just think of yourself as a protected by-product."

She found her lips curling in a smile, even under the worst circumstances imaginable: her daughter in danger, the ranch on the verge of bankruptcy and her unrelenting grandparents in her house for an indeterminate amount of time.

"Protected by-product? You sure do have a way with words, Scottie Boy. It's almost enough to make a girl's heart beat a little faster."

Ewen's own heart beat a little faster at her words. Was she flirting with him? Did he want that to be the case? Absolutely not! His thoughts must have been reflected in his face, because her smile melted away and she pushed herself away from the side of the house. His heart beat even faster at the millisecond of hurt in her eyes before she got back to business.

"Why don't you go work your magic on Minerva and Franklin and I'll check in with Bart."

At those dismissive words, he stood there a minute as she rounded the corner of the house, feeling as if he'd lost something important, but he shook off the sentiment. If Tempe was guilty of using the castle as a drop-off and pickup for vital information, she could be a traitor. But he'd seen no signs of anyone furtively contacting her, and she appeared to be what she presented to the world. But as he well knew, appearances could be deceiving. One woman in his past even claimed the child she was carrying belonged to him and he'd only ever met the woman a few times. His family's success and money were powerful lures.

He went through the side door and stepped back into the kitchen, only to find Riley talking up a storm. Both great-grandparents sat in chairs with dazed looks on their faces. Ewen hid a grin. If the older couple hadn't been around children in years, they had no idea what they were in store for. It might be a good thing for Riley's great-grandparents to stick around for a while. Ewen was very close to his parents and his grandfather, and couldn't imagine life without them. Maybe God was using this situation to heal the family.

Lost in his thoughts, he found his mind jerking back to the present when something Riley said caught his attention.

"—and Great-Gamy, I haven't told you the best part. You can help us find the gold."

Gold? What gold? Ewen knew something was up when Effie hopped out of her chair and started talking fast. "Why don't I make us a pot of coffee?" Ewen watched as she nervously grabbed a coffee canister out of the cabinet.

"And I have some cookies I baked yesterday from scratch. Does anyone want cookies with their coffee?"

Dudley pushed himself out of his chair and stepped over to Effie, laying one of his hands over hers, effectively calming her anxious movements. Ewen's chin dropped. Effie and Dudley? Impossible! They hadn't had time to get to know one another that well. Dudley was just helping, as was his wont.

Ewen cringed. Tempe was right. Even his thought vocabulary was unusual. It had to be the writer in him. But back to the gold. Before he could open his mouth to inquire, Tempe walked quickly through the arched opening leading off the foyer. He assumed the fire must be extinguished, as she evidently came through the front door. Her jaw was locked solid, telling him she must have overheard the conversation, but she managed a tight smile.

"Riley, why don't you show the Rodericks to your granddaddy's old room." She shot a hard look at the older couple. "Unless you've already made arrangements to stay elsewhere?"

Minerva shook her head, which told Ewen the older woman had probably assumed she'd march in, take Riley with her, and be on the next plane leaving Texas. He doubted they had planned to stay.

Ewen's suspicions about the "gold" slip were confirmed at the look of horror on Riley's face. "Mama, I didn't mean to say anything about the map and the gold. I just thought Great-Gamy and Great-PawPaw would like to help us hunt for it so we can save the ranch."

Minerva made a gurgling sound at Riley's nickname for her great-grandfather, but wisely didn't say anything.

"You're in danger of losing Riley's home?" she shrilled, and Ewen closed his eyes. This was going from bad to worse. This should be an opportunity of healing for the family, not a time of more strife.

He stepped into the fray. "Riley, your mother made a good suggestion. Take your great-grandparents upstairs and settle them in." He turned his suave sophistication on Minerva and Franklin. "The accommodations are a perfect representation of Western appeal. I think you'll enjoy the ambience."

Minerva snapped her mouth shut and slowly pulled herself to her feet. A surprised look crossed her face when Riley grabbed their hands.

"Come on, Gamy. Is it all right if I call you Gamy and PawPaw? It's a lot easier to say. Adding the 'great' is a real big mouthful."

Minerva and Franklin wore dazed expressions while accompanying her out of the room. Once they were out of earshot, Ewen turned on Tempe.

"Gold? You have a map leading to gold? Could that be why someone is trying to force you off your ranch? Is that why someone broke into your grandfather's study? You want my help, but you leave out something as important as a map leading to gold?" He should have stopped there, but couldn't help himself. "Or maybe someone wants what you took out of the castle library and destroying your farm is their way of forcing you to give it back."

A tight smile stretched across her face. Ewen found himself mourning the loss of the flirty, easy smile she'd bestowed upon him while leaning against the side of the house, but he swiped that emotion away. This was serious business. He knew he'd made a gross error when Tempe relaxed and studied him from head-to-foot, her gaze returning to his face.

"Well, now, Mr. Duncan, you've got that nice, big ole limousine squatting in my driveway. Why don't you just have your valet pack your bags and head on back to Scotland. I'll deal with me and mine."

Ewen's heart plummeted to his toes as he returned her bold, challenging stare. He *did not* want to leave! Because, because… Yes! Because he had to find out what she took from the library. It was a matter of national security, although he didn't think the video was sufficient evidence to call in his superiors at the DIA and have Tempe placed on a watch list. Or at least that was what he convinced himself of.

Dudley cleared his throat. Ewen had forgotten his valet and Tempe's aunt were still in the kitchen. "Sir, if I may suggest, why don't we table the discussion concerning what happened in Scotland and assist Ms. Calloway and her lovely aunt in finding the gold. Four heads are better than two and a positive result might save their ranch."

Ewen grasped onto that life preserver with both hands. He had to stay here. He glanced back at Tempe. "I was out of line. I apologize. I promised to help, and I will. Ned's men are en route as we speak. If you don't want to tell me about the map and gold, I can accept that."

Which wasn't quite true, because he had a burning desire to know exactly what was going on here. He wanted to squirm, but held his posture straight while awaiting her decision. It was her property and she could force him to leave if that was what she wanted.

Tempe sat and everyone followed suit.

"When he died three months ago, my grandfather's attorney gave me a…letter from Granddad, telling me about a map that leads to gold, and, yes, Dudley, it could save the ranch. Riley and I have searched for the gold, but the terrain drawn on the paper is off somehow and we haven't been able to find it." She gave Ewen another hard look. "Only me, Riley and Aunt Effie know about the map, as far as I know. But the gold could possibly be the motivation for the destruction around the ranch if someone else does know."

Ewen had to pose the question burning in his gut. "What if your grandfather told someone about the map? What if that person is willing to kill and maim to get their hands on the gold?" He hesitated because he was barely back in her good graces, but decided to ask anyway.

"Also, Tempe, you never did tell me how your grandfather died," he added.

TEN

The question about her grandfather's death stunned her.

"Maybe he did," Ewen said.

"Excuse me? Maybe he did what?" Tempe asked.

A fire lit Ewen's eyes, as if he was on to something, and perhaps he was. "Maybe your grandfather did tell someone else about it. Maybe that someone else got rid of your grandfather, hoping to force him into revealing information about the gold."

Horror mixed with hope warred within her. Horror at the idea that someone had killed her grandfather for monetary gain, and hope that the gold was actually real and could save the ranch. But what Ewen was suggesting couldn't be true. She couldn't accept that someone had committed murder for a map leading to gold. It wasn't possible. She started shaking her head and Ewen reached across the table to touch the back of her hand.

"Tempe, how did your grandfather die?"

She shook her head again in denial. "His name was Dillard Calloway. Everyone called him Dill." She smiled in remembrance. "He was stubborn and crotchety, but everyone who knew him loved him. No, you're wrong, his death was an accident. No one killed him."

Ewen rubbed little circles on the top of her hand, and somehow it felt comforting.

"What kind of an accident?" he asked gently.

When she lifted her head and gazed into his eyes, as dark as midnight blue sapphires, she detected nothing but concern.

"He was delivering supplies to our boys out on the range, not too far from the hot springs area where our chopper landed."

She concentrated on his fingers making smooth circles on her hand. It was better than thinking about the day her grandfather had died, leaving Tempe, Riley and Effie to go on without him. Her grandfather always made everything seem possible. He was so full of energy and he always claimed the Good Lord looked after him. Tempe didn't buy into that because half her family had been taken from her way too soon.

"Tempe?"

It took her a minute to recall the conversation. It was as if all the family hardships that had happened since she was seventeen years old—when her parents had died in a plane crash—had finally caught up with her. The pity in Ewen's gaze was what finally snapped her out of it. Jerking her hand out from beneath his, she got a grip on things. If someone had dared to kill her grandfather for gold, she'd find out who and make sure justice was served.

"As I said, he was out delivering supplies near the hot springs area for the boys. Bart was there when it happened. He said Granddad unloaded the supplies from his saddlebags, then started riding around the area. Bart didn't think anything of it because Granddad did that all the time.

"He heard Granddad's horse create a ruckus, like something was wrong, and by the time he mounted his own horse and caught up with him, my grandfather had been thrown. He died of a broken neck. Everyone assumed a snake or some wild animal spooked his mount."

The room went quiet until Ewen broke the silence. "Tempe, may I see the map your grandfather left you?"

Mixed emotions churned in Tempe's stomach. Her grandfather had left her a private letter with instructions on finding the map, which the attorney had presented after the reading of the will. He'd hidden it in a book at the ranch, one of the many books he loved so much.

Once she started looking for it, Aunt Effie

informed her she'd sold all the books with any value, which were quite a few. Tempe could never understand why he hadn't put the map in the safe like a normal person. It had taken a lot of effort to track down the buyer of that particular book, and a trip to Scotland wasn't cheap, but she had been desperate. They needed a large infusion of cash to save the ranch, and she'd hoped to find the map and the gold.

She shifted her eyes toward Ewen. If he ever found out the map was what she'd taken from his grandfather's castle, would he try and claim it since his family purchased the book from Aunt Effie through a broker? Squatter's rights and all that? Well, she'd never tell him what she'd retrieved from the castle because it was rightfully hers, so it shouldn't be a problem.

She went for a negligent shrug, even though she was wound up tighter than a clock, and stood up. "I'll get it out of the safe." All the way up the stairs, into the bedroom and while she was opening the old-fashioned safe, Ewen's words swirled around in her mind. Could her grandfather have been killed because of the map?

Reaching into the safe, which was hidden behind a picture of the Texas plains, she pulled out a zip baggie that held the paper. Pulling the slide open, she removed the document. She stared at the crude drawing and the *X* marked in red. As she had many times before, she examined the mountain range, which resembled the mountains hovering at a distance behind the hot springs. She and Riley had hunted for the place marked in red, but the terrain on the map was too vague and they hadn't been able to find it. Tempe smiled because those were fond memories. Riley's eyes would light up like a Christmas tree every time they searched for the gold.

She closed the safe and straightened the picture before bounding out of what she still considered her granddad's office, back down the stairs and into the kitchen. Holding the map out, she handed it to Ewen. "Okay, Scottie Boy, give it your best shot."

He gently took the paper, his fingers brushing hers, and gazed into her eyes. "I'll do my best."

She rocked back on her heels. "Well, you can start looking without me. I have to be in Florida at eight o'clock sharp tomorrow morning. Will Ned's men be here by then? They can look out for Riley and the grandparents while I'm gone."

That statement had Ewen gaping. "What?"

Aunt Effie chimed in. "I think it's a horrible thing, them putting her through this. I think you should have your sister come home."

Ewen shot Tempe a questioning look.

"No, Aunt Effie, Liv has enough on her plate right now. We'll handle this ourselves." She turned back to Ewen. "My psych eval. It's tomorrow morning. I have to be in Florida."

"And you're just now telling me about this?" Tempe's temper flared, but Ewen closed his eyes and made a good choice. "Let me rephrase that. It's fairly late in the day. What are your travel plans?"

Instead of answering, Tempe asked a previously unanswered question. "Will Ned's men arrive today?"

Ewen's phone beeped right at that moment. He pulled his cell out of his pocket and grinned. "Perfect timing. They just joined Simon out at the hot springs. I'll instruct them to watch over the house while we're gone."

"We? Who said you're going to Florida?"

He gave her a serious look. She actually didn't mind if he tagged along. It'd be good to have company to keep her mind off the upcoming evaluation, as long as everyone at the ranch was protected.

He cleared his throat. "I'd like to scope out the place, maybe ask a few questions while you're busy."

"Yeah? Questions about what?"

"You're positive the Blue Angel crash wasn't your fault, and after almost crash-landing with you and experiencing your flight expertise firsthand, I'm inclined to agree with you."

"They went over my jet with a fine-toothed comb, at least what was left of it. I doubt there's anything else to find."

"It won't hurt."

Since she'd already decided to let him tag along, she shrugged her shoulders again. "Suit yourself. Pack light. We won't be there long."

Two hours later, after Tempe had met and approved of Ned's men and said goodbye to Riley, Aunt Effie, Dudley and her unwanted guests, Ewen gaped as Tempe's truck came to a shuddering stop at the end of a long, paved driveway. The house that sat in front of them was a large white classical ranch house with a wide, wraparound porch. The tall, broad-shouldered man attired in Western clothing and the coon dog beside him on the top front porch step fit the scene. The one thing that didn't fit was the gleaming white Cessna resting on a dirt airstrip in the middle of a pasture to the left of the house.

"Sitting in front of us is my travel plan, to answer the question you asked me earlier," Tempe said, a gleam of anticipation lighting her eyes.

Ewen waged war with the rusted-out door until it finally creaked open. "Are you allowed to fly before your evaluation?"

She grinned, and his heart sang in response. It

was good to see her smile again, but he quickly doused the feeling.

"I have an up-to-date FAA private pilot's license. Have license, can fly."

He grunted. "Funny. I assume the cowboy standing on the porch steps owns the plane?"

She grinned when she opened her truck door with much more aplomb than he had. "Come on, I'll introduce you. There's a whole lot more to Mac Dolan than appears on the surface."

They strode across the pavement and stopped at the bottom of the steps.

"Ewen Duncan, meet Mac Dolan. Mac flew beside me in the Blue Angels my first year. After he finished his two-year term, he mustered out of the military and came home for good."

Ewen gave the man a critical assessment. Mac was decent-looking in a rugged, masculine kind of way. Quite the opposite of Ewen. Ewen more or less fit the James Bond mold. Was Tempe attracted to the rugged look, or did she like more of a suave appeal? Ewen shook his head. It didn't matter what kind of man she was attracted to. He wasn't here to date her.

Mac came down the steps and held out his hand. "Any friend of Tempe's is a friend of mine." Ewen shook his hand and Mac returned his attention to Tempe. "The Cessna's gassed up and ready to go. No need to hurry, I'm not planning on going anywhere."

Tempe nodded, then lifted her head. "I appreciate you letting me borrow it. You sure you trust me to—"

Mac held up a hand, effectively cutting her off. "I know your psych eval is tomorrow. I also know you've got a steel backbone when it comes to flying. You're the best of the best, so don't ask a stupid question like that again."

"Appreciate it," Tempe said, then gave him a quick salute and took long strides toward the plane. Ewen mumbled, "It was nice to meet you," and hurried after her. He climbed the stairs leading to the plane and barely made it in before the door started closing. The engines were revving by the time he sat in the copilot's seat and buckled himself in. The glitter in her eyes caused his stomach to flip-flop. The sensation got worse after she spoke.

"You ready to rock 'n roll, Scottie Boy?"

Ewen had seen the Blue Angels perform. He'd ridden in plenty of planes, including military planes, but they didn't have Blue Angel pilots at the helm. Blue Angels performed dangerous feats that seemed impossible. He prayed Tempe wouldn't decide to have a little fun on the way to Florida.

He gripped the armrest and stared down the

fairly short runway, but almost lost his lunch when Tempe released a shout.

"Hooyah!" she yelled, then pushed the yoke forward.

Her full concentration was glued to the runway in front of them, and he certainly didn't care to distract her at this particular moment. His stomach rebelled again as they reached the end of the runway and Tempe pulled the yoke all the way back. The nose of the plane was so far in the air that Ewen couldn't see anything but a clear sky out the front window. He took small breaths to hold the nausea in. No takeoff he'd ever experienced had had this much speed and momentum.

Tempe hollered again as the plane leveled off and Ewen's stomach settled a bit when he spotted land on the horizon.

"I take it you're glad to be in the cockpit of a plane again?" he asked, still gripping the armrest.

Her face was flushed and the widest grin he'd ever seen on her stretched across her face. He couldn't think of anything in his life that brought him as much joy as flying evidently brought her.

"You bet'cha! There's nothing like being in the air."

He couldn't imagine what it had done to her, being suspended from her Blue Angel status, but he was beginning to understand how much flying meant to her.

"You can unbuckle your seat belt now. We've reached altitude."

Ewen chose to stay safely buckled. "So you flew with Mac Dolan? Did you know him growing up?"

She shook her head. "Not really. Mac and his four brothers were older than me and Liv, so we weren't in school at the same time. They were known for being a boisterous bunch, although they all turned out pretty well. Mac and I really got to know each other in the Blue Angels. I was his wingman my first year."

Instead of worrying about how close Tempe and Mac were, it was time to get back to business. "You said there were those who didn't approve of female pilots in the Blue Angels. Do you think that's in any way connected to your crash or the things happening at the ranch?"

Tempe shook her head. "I don't see how it could be. True, it would be a good way to get rid of me, but we have heavy security at Forrest Sherman Field Air Station. It would have to be an inside job if anyone messed with my jet."

Ewen waited without answering. It didn't take long for the explosion to arrive.

"Oh, no. You're not going around questioning my teammates, accusing them of trying to kill me. Not a one of them would do that."

"Tempe, who doesn't like female pilots?"

Ewen disliked putting her through this, but as he well knew, information could come from the most unlikely place.

"My commanding officer, selected as the boss of my team by the chief of naval training, wasn't too keen when I got picked, but he got over it when I proved my flight skills."

He threw in a different question because it was weighing on his mind. "Are you nervous about your psych eval tomorrow morning?"

She didn't hesitate to answer. "Not one bit. Flying is in my blood, and the crash didn't affect my mental state at all as far as flying. Our helicopter incident confirmed that. The only thing I'm worried about is the psychologist. I don't like people probing into my mind and digging deep into my psyche. With me, what you see is what you get."

Ewen wasn't so sure of that, but he let it drop. In his opinion, Tempe had hidden layers he itched to peel back. Did she ever allow anyone close enough to connect on a more personal level? Which brought up another question.

"What about Riley's father? Is he in the picture and could he have anything to do with what's happening at the ranch?"

At first Tempe looked like she wanted to spit, then she rolled her shoulders and relaxed. "It's a common story. Michael was as young and stupid as I was. My parents had just been killed in a plane crash, and, I don't know, I guess it's like the old song says, I looked for love in all the wrong places. He split as soon as I told him I was pregnant."

"Has he ever tried to contact you?"

She shook her head. "He didn't grow up in Brewster County. His parents were visiting some of our neighbors for the spring and summer and they left when school started. I don't even know if he ever told them."

"What about child support?"

She shrugged. "We were both kids and I didn't have the money to take him to court. I decided Riley and I were better off without him."

Tempe suddenly stiffened, and Ewen gripped the armrests again. It reminded him of when they were in the chopper. "What is it?" he asked, already gritting his teeth in preparation for anything.

"I'm not sure, but the aircraft coming up on the left side of our plane shouldn't be flying that close. I filed a flight plan, and anybody with a lick of sense knows better than to get that close."

Ewen held his breath while Tempe attempted to contact the other plane via radio. When they didn't respond, she checked in with Air Traffic Control. She spouted off a bunch of numbers, then asked if anyone was cleared to fly near their coordinates.

Ewen gripped the armrest once again when ATC warned that no one should be in their general vicinity. Ewen became grim when Tempe said, "Well, I got a bogey on my tail. I'll let you know shortly if it's a friendly."

"Hang tight, Scottie Boy. We're gonna do a vertical roll with a half-loop and come up behind this boy, see what he's up to."

A vertical roll? A half-loop? Before he even had a chance to prepare for whatever that was, although he had a good indication by the names of the maneuvers, an ear-deafening noise filled the cockpit, followed by an odd shearing sound, then what sounded like an explosion. The plane gave one large shudder, and the control panel lit up like a Christmas tree.

ELEVEN

Her adrenaline pumping, Tempe shouted over all the noise. "Hold on! We lost an engine, but this sweet baby has a spare. A Rolls Royce engine, no less. Wish I had some firepower."

Tempe took a quick glance at Ewen. His face had lost all color, his eyes were closed, and his lips were moving. If she had to take a guess, she'd say he was praying. Praying wasn't going to save the day, but her flying skills would. She'd see to it.

After pointing the bird straight up in the air, she managed the control column, which moved the flaps on the wings, placing them into a roll. She reached the altitude she wanted, came back down in a half-loop and got on the tail of the bogey. She didn't know who was after them, and she didn't have any weapons onboard, but she'd pit her flying skills against them on any day.

Ignoring Ewen's gasp, she went into what she referred to as the "zone" when she was flying with the Angels. Nothing existed but her and the jet.

"Well, now, looks like you're flying a Cessna 172, buddy, and we're in a Citation, so that means we can outfly you."

Tempe felt the power of the Citation vibrate beneath her feet as she increased the speed and came alongside the 172. She moved the jet forward a bit further and physically peered into the other plane's front window. The pilot's head jerked around, eyes widened, but the face was hidden under a ski mask.

"That's right, buddy, you should be scared. Very scared," Tempe said, right before moving in so close she tapped the wing of her jet against his. She'd touched planes in the Blue Angels many times. It wasn't dangerous when she was performing with her teammates, but she didn't know how the other pilot would react, so she quickly put some distance between them. But not before seeing the pilot's mouth open in what she hoped was a scream.

"Uh-huh, you ain't seen nothin' yet, my friend."

"Wait! Please don't touch that plane again!" The firm command pierced the blanket of her concentration, and she glanced at Ewen's pale face and saw he'd pulled out one of the two computer keyboards in the cockpit, his fingers typing so fast they were almost a blur. The large moni-

tor on the copilot's side of the plane had a bunch
of numbers scrolling across it.

"Ned was recently in a situation similar to this
one, and I have an idea. I'm going to attempt to
take control of the opposing aircraft."

Adrenaline still pumping, Tempe said, "I take
it you didn't enjoy the ride?"

He gave her a one-second look. "Please tell me
our plane isn't on fire, or something of a dire nature that you're not telling me about."

"No problem. We're okay to fly. It's not like in
the movies. Most of these jets have self-contained
areas to protect the second engine."

Ewen typed furiously for another few seconds,
then sat back, intent on the computer screen. His
lips finally curved in a satisfied smile. "We have
control of the plane. Where would you like him
to land?"

When she didn't say anything, his eyes met
hers and she asked softly, "Just how does a fictional novelist know how to hack into another
jet's computer system?"

"Let's please land this plane and we can talk
later."

Oh, yeah, they'd talk later, because she had a
ton of questions. Before pulling away from the
other jet, she glanced one more time into the pilot's window and pushed the joystick sharply to
the left.

Ewen grabbed his armrests again. "What! What's wrong now?"

Gritting her teeth, Tempe stalled the jet to get far to the left and behind the other plane so she could verify what she thought he was planning to do. Sure enough, the guy ejected from the plane. She watched as he shot straight into the air, then started falling. By the time she circled back around, his parachute was carrying him safely to the ground.

"Ewen, have you ever heard the term autoland?"

His voice hoarse, Ewen asked, "Did that pilot just eject from his plane?"

"Ewen!" Tempe said more forcefully.

"Aye?" he said, finally focusing on her.

"Do you know what auto-landing is?"

"Nay!" It was amusing to Tempe that the stress of the situation caused Ewen to slip into his Scottish accent, far different from his normal, sophisticated speech. But really, considering the situation, he was doing pretty well.

"It means we're going to have to land that plane via computer. If we don't, it might crash and kill someone." He shook his head, but she kept talking. They had to make this work. "You can set the computer to auto-land, but you'll have to monitor everything very closely."

Ewen stared at her, then looked at the plane

flying in front of them. "I just thought to take control of the plane and force the pilot to land. I didn't think I'd be the one landing it."

"Ewen, we have no choice. It appears as if you're some kind of computer whiz, so see if you can figure out how to set the controls of the other plane to auto-land while I check in with ATC and let them know what's going on. Here are the co-ordinates," she said and rattled off the numbers.

She radioed Air Traffic Control at Forrest Sherman Field where they had planned to land and was stunned when the Chief Officer of the Blue Angels answered the call.

"Lieutenant Commander Tempe Calloway, what are you doing flying a plane? You're supposed to be grounded," he snapped out. Tempe cringed. She ignored Ewen's sharp look and straightened her shoulders as if she was standing in front of the admiral.

"Sir, technically I'm grounded by the military, but I do have a civilian's pilot's license, which still allows me to fly."

She heard a heavy sigh filter through the mic. Admiral Brawley had always been a tough old bird, but he was fair and he'd never had a problem with her being a woman.

"What's your plan?"

"Sir, I have a civilian computer expert on-board—" Ewen cut her a sharp glance and she gave him a saucy grin "—and he's going to set the computer on the 172 to auto-land. He'll monitor the situation from our onboard computer. I'll follow the plane in to make sure everything goes according to plan."

"Fine. Our guys will monitor it from here. And Temper?" Ewen frowned at the nickname.

"Yes, sir?"

"No hotdoggin' it. A nice safe landing is what we're going for here."

Tempe grinned. "Yes, sir!"

Ewen's fingers paused on the keyboard. "Temper?"

Tempe shrugged. "I give as good as I get when the boys rag me about being a woman." She pointedly looked at the computer screen. "Please tell me you can set the other jet to auto-land."

"Maybe. Probably. Give me a few minutes."

"No worries, we have ten minutes or so before reaching the landing strip."

Ewen mumbled something, but his fingers moved quickly over the keyboard. She kept her eyes on the plane in front of them until Ewen finally leaned back in his seat, a bead of sweat rolling down his forehead.

"I think I have it."

"You think? Can't you give me a little more than that?"

"How about you tell me what you took in Scotland and I'll see if I can do better," he snapped.

Tempe realized she'd pushed him too far. For a civilian, this was a stressful situation, so she cut him a little slack. "Listen, you've done a great job. Just keep a close eye on your monitor and tell me everything that's happening. We'll be ready to land the plane shortly."

He sniffed in that aristocratic way he had and turned his attention to the monitor. They stayed quiet until his computer started beeping.

"Okay," Tempe said, "the plane needs to start descending from cruising altitude. I'm going to talk you through it, and you make sure the other plane is doing what I say."

"Fine," he snapped. "The plane is descending."

"You're doing good, Ewen. The approach guidance, known as the Instrument Landing System, gives the lateral position relative to the runway. It'll tell us if the plane is on the proper slope—the descension slope. I need those numbers."

He rattled off the numbers and Tempe took a relieved breath when she realized the jet was on a three-degree slope. So far, so good.

"Okay, the plane should be decreasing speed."

"It is."

"About now the flaps and slats should be deploying."

She held her breath as Ewen studied the monitor, then said, "Good to go."

The ATC had been calling out the height above the runway in her radio and she confirmed. They were almost to twenty feet.

"Ewen, are the throttles closing on the plane?"

"Yes."

Tempe saw the nose of the aircraft lift and held her breath until the plane hit the runway, confirming the landing gear had dropped. She flew over it, then circled back around and was able to see the jet come to a complete stop. Fire trucks and emergency vehicles filled the runway and she grinned. Slapping Ewen on the shoulder, she let out a loud whoop.

"Ewen, we did it! We landed the plane."

He turned his head away from the computer screen and very calmly said, "Please put this plane on autopilot."

Snapped out of her adrenaline-rush euphoric state, she asked, "What?"

"Put. The. Plane. On. Autopilot."

Tempe was confused and worried that maybe he'd snapped from the stressful situation, and did as he asked.

"Is the plane on autopilot?"

"Yes. Ewen, are you okay?"

"No, I'm not okay. You're a dangerous woman

to spend time with, and if I'm going to die because of it, I'm not going without this first."

He leaned in slowly across the aisle between the seats, and when his lips stopped a breath away from hers, she realized what he was about to do and closed the gap between them, immediately becoming lost in the sweetest kiss she'd ever had in her life.

Confused and a tad upset by her own unexpected response, she slowly opened her eyes, but snapped to alert when she felt a light tap on the outside of her plane. As she peered out the side window, her stomach dropped, and she groaned.

"What now?" Ewen asked, his voice filled with trepidation.

Tempe leaned back and pointed her thumb at her side window. "Look for yourself."

Ewen leaned forward with a quizzical expression. "I assume those are some of your teammates in that plane alongside us, but what in the world are they doing. It almost looks as if they're kissing air, smacking their lips like that."

"They saw us kissing and I'm sure there'll be photos to pass around so the boys can rib me."

Ewen cleared his throat. "Tempe, about that kiss—"

She held up a hand, effectively shutting him up.

"It was nothing. We just experienced a harrowing experience and all that. Forget about it."

Before Ewen could respond, Tempe's radio came to life. "Lieutenant Commander, get your plane on the ground. Now!"

Tempe snapped to at the admiral's sharp command. "Yes, sir!" Nothing like reality slapping her in the face after experiencing a kiss that almost knocked her socks off.

Ewen heaved a big sigh of relief when the Cessna finally came to a stop on the runway. With quick, practiced movements, Tempe unbuckled her harness and stood, before Ewen even had a chance to get his bearings after that ordeal. The fire of a battle won lit her eyes and energy crackled around her. The woman was truly amazing.

"You did good, Scottie Boy. Now step it up because I'm sure the admiral's waiting on the tarmac, ready to ream me out."

He grabbed her hand before she could leave the cockpit. "Later, we're going to talk about that kiss."

She shrugged as if it wasn't a big deal, and for some reason that didn't sit well with him. He should be happy it didn't mean anything to her, because there couldn't ever be anything between them. She was keeping secrets, and so was he.

Unhooking his harness, he followed her out of the plane. By the time his feet hit the ground, Tempe was standing at attention in front of a man he assumed to be Admiral Brawley. The admiral had the perfect military presence, with a trim body outfitted in a high-ranking uniform. Silver winged his temples, showcasing his black hair, and his mouth was moving at a rapid speed.

Ewen chuckled. It appeared as if Tempe was correct in expecting what she called a "reaming out." He headed in their direction, and when he reached hearing distance, the one-way conversation halted.

Tempe nodded at Ewen as he stopped beside her.

"Sir," she said, "this is Ewen Duncan. He helped auto-land the 172."

Admiral Brawley pierced Ewen with intelligent, laser-sharp cobalt blue eyes and gave a short nod. "We appreciate your help. You'll need to be debriefed along with Lieutenant Commander Calloway."

Ewen grinned at Tempe. It was interesting to see her in a different element as compared to the cowgirl at the ranch. "Happy to do my part."

And mystifyingly enough, he found he was feeling happy, which didn't make any sense after the experience he'd just undergone. Even with the thrill of analyzing and interpreting data for the DIA, he was stunned to realize he'd been somewhat dissatisfied with his life. Not that he wanted to spend a lifetime with a woman as adventurous as Tempe, or any woman, for that matter, but it did open his eyes.

The admiral dismissed them, but just as they turned to walk away, Brawley raised his voice. "And Temper, good job getting the 172 on the ground in one piece."

Tempe gave her boss a wide grin and Ewen's heart lifted even more. The debriefing didn't take but an hour or so, and when they left the building, Tempe took long strides toward another smaller building.

"It's getting late. Shall we pick up some dinner and locate a hotel?"

She came to a sudden stop and pivoted on her heel, facing him. "Listen, Ewen, you did real good up there today, and I appreciate it, but you were right when you said we need to talk, mainly about where you came across those way-above-average computer skills, but first we have to get something over with."

She strode forward again and Ewen easily kept pace with her. "We've been debriefed. What else is there?"

She pointed toward the front of the smaller building they were approaching. "You'll see."

Bursting with curiosity, Ewen followed her through the door and had to allow his eyes time to adjust to the darkened interior. A huge, extensive bar filled an entire wall and tables were scattered throughout the room.

He had just noted thirty or so men gathered in the room when the lights went out and a large screen hanging on the wall blasted to life with a picture. A picture of him kissing Tempe in the Cessna midair.

A big, booming voice broke the silence. "Not only can Tempe fly and land a plane on auto-land, she can kiss while she's doing it."

The whole room erupted with laughter and ribbing as the lights came back on. Tempe rocked back on her heels and grinned.

"Not that any smart woman would ever get close enough to any of you knuckleheads to kiss you, but if you ever find yourself in that position, now you know how it's done."

There was a lot of good-natured teasing and backslapping, and she finally raised a hand. "Now, all kidding aside, what happens in the Blue Angels stays in the Blue Angels. I don't think the admiral would appreciate seeing my face splattered all over social media kissing Ewen Duncan."

The room went deathly quiet, and all eyes focused on him as if he'd just walked into the room versus having been standing there the whole time. A lone voice asked, "You're the writer and Bachelor of the Year?"

Ewen nodded, and just like that, he became one of the boys. He took advantage of the situation and used his subtle skills to interrogate each and every one of Tempe's flying mates. It was very interesting what he managed to discover.

TWELVE

After catching a lift from one of the guys and renting two rooms at a local hotel, Tempe stared at Ewen from across the table of an Italian restaurant down the street from their digs. She leaned back in her chair and crossed her arms over her chest, but before she could ask her first question, her cell rang. Tugging it out of her jeans pocket, she stared at the screen for a second. Should she answer right now? She could always call her back later. She answered.

"Hey, sis. What's up?"

"*What's up?* Why don't you tell me? I just received a text from one of your rowdy Blue Angel buddies. It's a picture of you kissing some guy in the cockpit of a plane. As far as I know, you've barely dated since Riley was born, and now I'm getting a picture of you kissing a guy I haven't even met? I just spoke with you four days ago and you didn't mention a man." Her voice rose in volume the longer she talked.

Tempe avoided looking at Ewen and lowered her head with the phone pressed to her ear, twisting sideways in her seat.

"Liv, it's nothing. Just the guys fooling around, giving me a hard time."

Silence, but not for long. Her sister hadn't become an international attorney by staying quiet. "So you didn't kiss this guy in the cockpit of an airplane?" Trust Liv to cut to the heart of the matter.

"Well, actually the picture is real." Before her sister had a chance to grill her, Tempe cut the conversation short. "It's a long story. I'll call you later and we'll talk."

Liv's voice lowered. "You're with him now, aren't you?"

"Yep."

"Okay, okay, just tell me his name."

"Ewen Duncan."

"*What?* The famous writer? The guy who was voted Bachelor of the Year? *That* Ewen Duncan? What in the world is he doing at your ranch?" Her voice had risen in volume again.

"Our ranch."

"What?"

"Liv, you own half of the ranch."

"I don't care about that. I want to know what's going on with you. Isn't your psych eval tomorrow morning?"

The focus was on Tempe, but she detected an underlying worry in Liv's voice.

"Liv, is something wrong?"

A longer silence, which in itself was highly unusual. "Not really. Just a few things going on at work. Nothing I can't handle."

Tempe believed her. Liv had a very high IQ, which she was very proud of. Her sister was smart as a whip.

"Okay, I'll call you later."

"Make sure that you do, and I'll be praying your evaluation goes well," Liv said and hung up.

Tempe slid the phone into her pocket, turned back around and straightened in her seat.

"Sorry about that. It was my sister."

"No problem. I understand. I have a brother."

The waiter approached the table and took their orders. Tempe went all out with lasagna, heavy on the meat, and Ewen ordered something called fritto misto. One of the many things different about them. Tempe was a steak and potato girl, while Ewen dined on caviar.

Her phone rang again, and Tempe pulled it out of her pocket. This time she had a smile on her face when she answered. It was Riley. Her daughter had her laughing in no time at all. After a few minutes, she wished Riley good-night and ended the call.

"Is everything okay at the ranch?"

"So far, so good. I wouldn't have left, psych eval or not, if Ned's men hadn't been there." She grinned. "Riley thought it was a good idea to show her gamy and pawpaw the ranch. From the sound of it, my illustrious, high-in-the-instep grandparents are trekking all over the ranch with Riley, getting up close and personal with the cattle and horses." Tempe laughed out loud and it felt good. "I'd love to be a fly on the wall, watching that."

Ewen lifted one of those perfectly groomed brows. "I can only imagine."

Tempe relaxed, leaned forward and propped her elbows on the table. "So where did you acquire enough computer skills to hack into a jet?"

He shrugged and Tempe's gut told her he wouldn't outright lie, but he wouldn't tell the whole truth, either.

"Ned and I both have a natural inclination toward technology. He used his skills in the CIA, and I've used mine in writing. A lot of my characters have advanced technical skills."

She leaned back in her chair. Okay, so he wanted to dance around the question. Time to change the subject. "Did you discover anything while interrogating my teammates?"

Surprise crossed his face. "You're observant."

"Yeah, it's kinda helpful to know what's going on around you when you're flying at twice the speed of sound, eighteen inches apart from five other jets."

With sophisticated flair, Ewen lifted his water glass to her. "An amazing feat. I'd love to see you fly with the Blues."

"If everything goes well tomorrow and I pass the psych eval, I'll be able to finish my last three months."

"Are you worried?"

"Not really. I'd like to finish, but I've already decided to muster out afterward so I can spend more time with Riley."

Ewen leaned forward. "Several of the men you work with had the same opinion as your commanding officer, Commander Paige. He doesn't favor female pilots being in the program. Tempe, he has access to all the planes. He could have sabotaged your jet."

Tempe was already shaking her head. "He doesn't like me, but he'd never risk his career because of that. I'll be gone in three months anyway, if I pass the psych eval. It doesn't make sense. And added to that, they detailed the jet, looking for mechanical failure. Nothing was found."

"Could discrediting you help discourage future women from wanting to fly with the Angels? And was Commander Paige part of the jet-detailing process?"

Tempe's stomach pitched and rolled at the idea.

"Ewen, Paige flies the number one jet for our team. As I said, we're traveling at supersonic speed and have to trust each other. The maneuvers we perform are life-threatening if any one of us is off our game. Everything we do is critically timed. Thankfully, my crash didn't hurt anyone else, but it could have."

Ewen didn't respond, just picked up his fork and started eating. "On a happier note, tonight, I'll take a look at the map you gave me and see if I can come up with a location for the gold."

Tempe grinned, glad to change the subject. "We've searched. You think you can do better? Go for it!"

They ate their dinner and made light conversation for the rest of the meal, which settled Tempe's stomach. Ewen insisted on paying and they left the restaurant with full stomachs and smiles on their faces.

The restaurant was built with only a sidewalk separating it from the street, and just as Tempe turned to say something to Ewen, he suddenly pushed her back toward the side of the building.

It was then she noticed a car had driven onto the sidewalk, straight toward them, and was now speeding away. "Tempe, are you okay?"

The worry in his voice warmed a place inside her that had been cold for a very long time. No one ever worried about her. She always took care of everyone else.

"I'm okay."

Ewen placed both hand on her shoulders.

"You still think no one in the Blue Angels wants you dead?"

Ewen's heart was beating wildly against his chest. He'd happened to spot the car at the last second and had automatically reacted to the danger. It wasn't an accident. The vehicle had swerved in an attempt to run Tempe down. Fear, anger and adrenaline had him popping out the first thing to enter his mind, and he shouldn't have. It was inappropriate timing.

"Tempe, I'm sorry. Forget I asked. We need to get you back to the hotel. A nice, soothing, hot bath is what you need."

People had gathered on the sidewalk, asking if they were okay, and Ewen took control of the situation. "Did anyone see the driver, or happen to get a license plate number? Make and model of the car?"

The small crowd murmured among themselves, but no one stepped forward with information. Tempe touched his arm and drew his attention.

"Let's get out of here."

"Do you want to call the police?"

She shook her head. "There's nothing they can do. Let's go."

Ewen studied her a moment and nodded. He took her hand, placed it in the crook of his arm and gained a smile from her. His heart finally settled down.

"Very British, Scottie Boy, but I can walk on my own."

He smiled back. "Have you ever thought I might be the one who needs the comfort and security of a personal touch?"

She angled her head up at him and this time he was gifted with a half grin. For some reason her smiles were becoming very important to him.

"Somehow, I don't believe that to be the case, but if it makes you feel better, I'll hang on to you until we get to the hotel."

They walked in comfortable silence. He'd never experienced that with a woman before. Most ladies wanted to impress him with either their beauty or their brains, but Tempe, attired in jeans, a Western shirt and cowboy boots, without a stitch of makeup on, didn't seem to care about any of that. She appeared to be comfortable in her own skin. Completely without artifice.

Soon, they were standing in front of her room. She pulled her arm free of his but didn't step away. She raised her head and peered at him. He felt as if he was being judged in some way, as if she was trying to figure him out. He leaned forward, close enough to kiss her, but a warning started beating in his head. What was he doing? The most sophisticated women in the world had tried to unscrupulously trap him into a relationship, and Tempe was far from proving herself trustworthy in his estimation. And there was the added fact that she lived in Texas and he spent a lot of his time in Scotland.

He pulled back and a flash of something—hurt?—passed across her eyes, but she stepped back and nodded briskly. "You saved my life back there on the sidewalk. I appreciate it."

What he really wanted to do was to pull her close and press his lips against hers, but he restrained himself. "You're welcome." He patted his pocket. "I have the map. I'll take a look at it and see what I can come up with."

"Good. That's good. I'm going to bed early, so I'll be ready for tomorrow."

She unlocked her door and disappeared without looking back. Almost of its own accord, his hand raised to knock on her door, but he slowly lowered it. For some reason, he felt as if he'd lost something important, something life-altering, but forced himself to walk away. Once in his room—right next to hers—he closed and locked the door behind him, leaned against it and shut his eyes.

The flash of hurt in Tempe's eyes played itself

over in his mind and he knew he would remember it for a long time to come. But what if she was a traitor to her country, a carrier used for transferring information? But why use the castle in Scotland? Maybe someone else was supposed to buy the book she removed the item from, but his grandfather somehow got to it first.

Lifting his briefcase off the sofa where he'd dropped it after they checked in, he opened a secret compartment and pulled out his personalized smartphone. He had a regular phone he carried on him, but he didn't want anyone listening in on this conversation. He tapped in the number and waited for the clicks. It was answered on the third ring.

"Dundar Castle."

Ewen had a moment of homesickness when he heard the old butler's familiar voice. "Alfred, it's Ewen."

"Master Ewen, 'tis so good to hear from you. Can I take it things are going well in the great state of Texas?"

Ewen frowned. He'd always wondered how Alfred knew so much, but now wasn't the time to question the older man.

"As well as can be expected. Is Grandfather in?"

"Yes, hold the line, please."

His grandfather came on the line. "Aye, I'd like

to know what my heir apparent is doing in Texas," his grandfather said in a gruff voice. Did everyone know he came to Texas?

"Grandfather, I'm not the heir to your title, Dad is. And it's only a title now, with no real power behind it."

He huffed. "That's what ye think, my boy, but ye're wrong."

It was an old argument. The family's successful art galleries were the only reason the castle was still in the family. "Listen, I have an important question."

"Aye, I'm listening."

Ewen would have to be careful not to give away too much information, because his grandfather was sharp as a tack. The name of the book Tempe had removed an item from had shown up on the security video, but it didn't reveal what she'd removed and slipped into her pocket.

"I'd like some information about a book you bought. It's Ernest Hemingway's *Death in the Afternoon*."

"Aye, 'tis a nice book, but only a tenth edition."

"Where did you purchase it?"

Sly as a fox, his grandfather asked, "And why is it important for ye to know?"

Ewen pinched his nose in frustration, praying for patience. "Please, Grandfather, just tell me where you got the book."

"Might this have something to do with that American organization ye work for? The DIA, ye call it?"

Ewen's eyes flew open wide. "How do you know about that?" he asked tightly.

His grandfather chuckled gruffly. "I tell ye, it pays to be laird of a castle. I know a lot of things."

He'd deal with that later. Right now, he wanted information. "The book?"

"Fine. Keep yer secrets. As ye know, I have contacts all over the world watching for rare editions. One of my fellow booklovers happened across this edition while browsing a store in— well, now, isn't this interesting now that I think on it. He found the book in a small bookstore in Texas while he was vacationing, and that's where ye'd be now. I called the store, purchased the book and had it mailed to me."

Ewen's stomach dropped. The book coming from Texas meant Tempe might somehow be involved.

"I appreciate it. And I'll be by to see you soon."

Before he could disconnect, his grandfather grumped. "It's high time ye moved back to the castle permanently."

Ewen ended the call and put away his phone. Rather than dwelling on the fact that Tempe might be guilty of serious crimes, he pulled the map from his pocket and sat at the small desk provided in the room. Turning on the lamp, he laid the old piece of paper out and smoothed it flat. It appeared to have been handled quite a bit. Ewen smiled thinking of Tempe and her daughter searching for gold.

He studied the crudely drawn map and tried to visualize the topography of the areas of the ranch he'd ridden on with Tempe. He wasn't an expert cartographer, but he did analyze information for the DIA. He turned the map to different angels, trying to gain multiple perspectives. It looked like part of the map included the foothills of the mountains, but it was missing something.

Frustrated, he held the map up to the lamplight, and then it hit him. A wide grin stretched across his mouth as he realized what he was looking at.

THIRTEEN

Tempe came wide-awake in an instant and held up her wrist, checking the time on her multifunction watch. It was 6 a.m. She had two hours before her evaluation. She closed her eyes, hoping to catch another thirty minutes of sleep, but soon realized that wasn't going to happen.

She'd just slipped her arms through the sleeves of the robe provided by the hotel, covering up her raggedy old pajamas, when someone knocked on her door. She peered through the peephole and there stood Ewen, a grin on his face. She really didn't feel up to sparring with him this morning, but she'd never considered herself a wimp, so she opened the door. The aroma of coffee hit her first and she grabbed his arm, pulling him into the room.

Staring at the two large cups he held in his hand along with a white paper bag of something that smelled delicious, she said, "Please tell me one of those is for me. If it's not, you might have a fight on your hands."

He held out a covered cup, and she grabbed it, ripped the lid off and took a big swallow. She closed her eyes as the caffeine hit her system, then opened them again. "I could almost kiss you for that."

As soon as the words were out of her mouth, she wanted to snatch them back, because Ewen had had plenty of opportunity to kiss her last night and he'd chosen not to. He'd kissed her on the spur of the moment in the jet, but his actions last night proved he'd reconsidered the situation. He wasn't interested, and neither should she be. She covered her humiliating slip the only way she knew how. "I'd kiss a skunk for a strong cup of morning coffee."

He knew what she was doing—she could see it in his eyes—but thankfully, he let it go and held up the white paper bag. "I also brought bagels. I thought you'd appreciate something to eat before your evaluation."

Even though Tempe had told him she wasn't anxious about the psych eval, her stomach pitched at the thought of food. She placed the coffee on the desk and tightened her robe.

"I appreciate it, but I better get showered and dressed."

Ewen's hand lifted and moved toward her, but

he dropped his arm. It was for the best. She had secrets and she suspected he did, too.

He stared at her for a second, but instead of leaving, he surprised her and took a seat on the sofa, patting the cushion. "Have a seat. You have plenty of time to get dressed, and I have some exciting news to share. Something that will hopefully cheer you up."

"Ewen, I—"

"It's about the map."

That came out of left field, but then she recalled he'd planned to look at the map last night. She grabbed her coffee and sat down beside him with an inward sigh. "Ewen, I appreciate you looking at the map, but Riley and I know that ranch like the back of our hands and we've never been able to find any gold."

He pulled the map out of his pocket and carefully smoothed it out on the coffee table. "That's because you didn't have the whole map."

That took her by surprise. She looked at the map, then back at Ewen. "I don't understand. This is the only map I'm aware of." She had to be careful talking about it. She didn't want Ewen asking too many questions. If there really was gold, his family might claim the rights to it because his grandfather had bought the book the map was hidden in.

His eyes lit with excitement as he hurried

over to the desk and moved the lamp so the light reached the coffee table. Holding the paper up to the light, he grinned. "Look and see for yourself."

She squinted at the map and shook her head. "I don't see anything. Listen, Ewen, I know you mean well, but what if there isn't any gold?"

He shook the paper in front of the light. "Let's take a different approach. Close your eyes and visualize the topography of the foothills at the base of the mountains on your ranch, then open your eyes and look at the map."

"Fine, anything to get this over with." She would never admit it, but she was getting antsy and wanted the evaluation over with. But she dutifully closed her eyes and envisioned the land she knew so well, then opened them and stared at the map. Suddenly, everything became clear.

"It's not all there. Some of the hills are missing."

"Very good," he said, sounding like a prim schoolteacher.

"But why the lamp? You could have done the same thing with it lying on the table."

"True, but holding it to the light is what made me realize there's another map."

"Another map?"

"Yes," he said, excitement thrumming in his voice. "This is what's called a map tableau. A crude one, but it makes sense."

His excitement was contagious. "Explain."

"To put it simply, it's a layered map. It's supposed to be laid on top of another one to get the whole effect. Today, while you're in your evaluation, I'll take it to a store and get it copied onto a clear sheet with the outlines of the map showing so it can be laid over a secondary map."

Her excitement dwindled as fast as it'd come. "And put it on top of what? I don't have another map."

"Tempe, there is another map, I'm sure of it. You said your grandfather drew the map and left it to you when he died. You need to search the house and see if you can locate the second one."

If only he knew. She'd turned the house upside down looking for the first map until Aunt Effie finally remembered she'd sold the book her grandfather had hidden it in, which led Tempe to Scotland. Hoping to avoid a deeper conversation about the map, she stood and forced a smile, her excitement dampened because she'd been all over the house and there was no second map.

"We'll search for it when we get home. I appreciate you taking a look at it."

He stood and faced her, placing a hand on her shoulder. "I was hoping to cheer you up with the news. I know you'll do great at the evaluation."

Tempe took a step back and his hand fell away. She forced her lips up at the edges. "Thanks.

We'll meet back up after the psych eval. I'll see if I can hitch us a ride home. I dread telling Mac about his plane."

Ewen studied her intently for a moment, then finally nodded. "Don't worry, I'm sure he has insurance. I'll check us out of the hotel, and after I make a copy of the map, I'll come back to the base and wait on you."

He left and Tempe stood there a moment, wishing that things could be different, but they weren't, so she marched to the bathroom and took her shower. After drying her hair, she unpacked her service dress uniform and slipped it on. She might be on leave, but she was still active in the military. Staring at herself in the mirror, she threw back her shoulders and made for the door. No matter what happened, she would face the world with her head up. Her plane crash wasn't due to human error and she had nothing to be ashamed about.

Ewen used the visitor's pass he'd been given the day before to get back on base and was directed to the building where she was having her evaluation. He told the receptionist he was waiting on Tempe and she pointed to a chair in the common room.

It was solid wood and extremely uncomfortable. The lady at the desk snuck furtive glances in his direction and he wanted to flash his DIA credentials as reassurance that he wasn't a terrorist. Pulling out the map, he studied it once again and assessed everything that had happened during the short time he'd been in Texas, and then Florida.

The explosion at her barn, the intruder inside her house, Riley's horrendous kidnapping, someone trying to shoot down the dilapidated helicopter, getting shot at on horseback, the sick cattle, the front porch fire, the terrifying experience in the jet on the trip to Florida, and then someone trying to run Tempe down with a car.

Whoever wanted her dead had far-reaching arms, which meant they had money and power. Tempe's grandparents had recently come onto the scene threatening to sue for custody of Riley. They definitely had money and power. Would someone in the Blue Angels go to such lengths to keep her out of the program and have her finish her term with the Angels in disgrace, hoping to discourage women in the future from joining?

And the map! Did someone burn her barn and break into her house to steal the map? Might there be multiple culprits?

All his thoughts came to a screeching halt and his brain ceased to function when a door opened and closed and Tempe came striding down the hallway with a grin splitting her face. But it wasn't the smile that made him feel like he'd been punched in the gut. He watched her move forward and knew he'd remember this moment for the rest of his life, until he was a very old man.

Her long, dirty-blond hair pulled back in a ponytail swished side to side as she took confident steps forward, and her eyes, as green as sparkling new grass after a nourishing rain, shone as bright as the sun.

She was decked out in a blue uniform with two yellow stripes on the left side running from shoulder to waist. Yellow highlighted her rank and name with the number three to the side. LCDR Tempe Calloway. Over her right chest was the Blue Angel patch signifying her unit, and an American flag was sewn to her left sleeve, close to her shoulder.

She was magnificent.

She stopped in front of him and propped her hands on her waist. In that moment, he really wanted to trust her, but he didn't dare.

"Well, aren't you gonna ask how it went?"

He snapped out of his reverie and grinned. "I take it the psychologist gave you the green light?"

"Yep," she said, her voice laced with satisfaction. "They figured if I was able to land the Cessna, along with an unmanned plane, I should be able to finish my three months with the Angels."

Excitement vibrated off her, and Ewen stood

still, mesmerized by her vitality and energy. Attraction for the woman began to grow in him, but he shook it off, although he allowed himself to celebrate this moment with her.

"That's super!" he said, and meant it. "When will you start back?"

Her enthusiasm dimmed. "The admiral expects me here in three weeks." Those imploring green eyes zeroed in on him. "If you really want to help me find out who's creating havoc in my life, now would be a good time."

Satisfaction flowed through him. He was completely in. He'd help Tempe find out who was trying to destroy her life, and at the same time he'd figure out what she'd been after at the castle.

"Well, then, let's get to it."

"I like your style, Scottie Boy. I hitched us a ride home, so we'll be there before suppertime." When he frowned, she snickered. "Don't worry, I'm not piloting. No fancy flying this time."

He shook his head. "I wasn't worried," he said, then gave her a wry smile. "I'm simply not fond of getting shot at while in the air."

He picked up his duffel and followed her out the door. "Where's your bag?"

She tossed her answer over her shoulder. "Dougie picked it up and took it to the plane."

He hurried to catch up with her. "Someone

named Dougie is flying the plane? That doesn't sound like a proper pilot's name."

She laughed again and it lightened his heart. What was it about this woman? She was creating havoc inside him. He didn't trust her, but found himself wanting to, and therein lay the danger.

They hitched a ride to the airstrip in a military jeep, boarded and were soon in the air. Dougie ended up being a clean-cut military guy, and Ewen was surprised when Tempe told him Admiral Brawley himself had authorized her ride home, in part because the military plane had a destination and they happened to be on the same route. The noise on the aircraft prevented conversation, and Ewen breathed a sigh of relief when the tires hit the ground at Mac Dolan's ranch.

Tempe spoke to Dougie before they deboarded and solemnly approached Mac, who was waiting outside.

"Mac, about your Cessna—"

He held up a hand. "I've already been contacted. It wasn't your fault that someone tried to take you down, and from what I hear, you're quite the hero for landing the 172. Don't worry, I have insurance."

Bold and proud as ever, Tempe looked him in the eye. "I don't know what your financial situation is, and it's none of my business, but if the insurance doesn't cover everything, send me a bill. I'll do my best to pay it, but it might have to be in installments."

Mac shook his head. "I'm fine, and I have very good insurance."

Tempe nodded, then added, "I didn't land the 172, Ewen did."

Mac shot him a surprised look, but it turned to speculation the longer they stood there.

"Is that so?" he drawled.

In that moment, Ewen realized Tempe was right. There was much more to Mac Dolan than he presented on the surface. When this whole thing was over, he'd be interested in finding out more about the man.

Tempe said her goodbyes. When they were in the rusted truck and bouncing their way home, a thought crossed his mind. "Has Mac ever offered to purchase your ranch?"

Tempe put that suspicion to rest quickly. "Nope, not one time. Mac's ranch has been in his family for as long as mine. Our grandfathers got along well."

"Tempe, I'm glad that your psych eval went well, and I feel as if we should celebrate the moment, but if you go back in three weeks, time is of the essence."

She nodded. "Go on."

"Well, while you were busy, I assessed all the

events that have happened since I've been at the ranch and came up with a few possibilities."

"Okay, let's hear what you've got."

Ewen liked her matter-of-fact response. He admired that even though she was fiercely independent, she was intelligent enough to know when to be a team player.

"To be able to come after you in Texas and follow us to Florida, our villain must have money, power and far-reaching contacts."

She grinned, and his attention was thrown off course once again.

"I don't find any humor in that statement," he said.

"It's that James Bond thing again. You used the word *villain*. I would've called them a low-down dirty rat."

He smiled back. "And there's the Annie Oakley we all know and love so well."

Her smile slid away, and he cleared his throat, getting back to the subject instead of explaining his verbal slip. "Yes, well, it occurred to me that your grandparents happened upon the scene rather suddenly, and they definitely have the money and power to hire people to do their bidding. But the map throws another kink into the picture. Their motive could be custody of Riley, as they don't need the money. What if they're trying to prevent you from attaining the map that would save your ranch?

"Then there's the Blue Angels. Would someone try to destroy you to discourage future female pilots? And then there's your neighbor, Thomas Hildebrand. He offered to purchase your land."

Her hands gripped the steering wheel, but she stayed ominously quiet. Ewen couldn't imagine how it would feel suspecting family members of trying to kill their own.

"Instinct tells me that locating the other part of the map may be one way to bring the culprits to the surface, or at least eliminate the map as being a reason for trying to get rid of you and destroy your ranch."

She gripped the steering wheel so tightly her knuckles whitened. "You don't understand," she said between clenched teeth.

"Then tell me." Frustration ate at him. His gut screamed that everything happening was related to her visit in Scotland, but he couldn't fit the pieces of the puzzle together.

Her eyes flashed with frustration when she glanced at him before turning back to the road. "I searched everywhere, and I only found the map you have. There is no other map."

FOURTEEN

Tempe wanted to scream in frustration. Everything she'd done to get the first map, even traveling to Scotland, was all for nothing, because she had no idea where a second map could possibly be. For the hundredth time, she wondered why her grandfather didn't tell her about the map and the gold before he died. Could everything at the ranch be happening because of the map?

She slid a sideways glance at Ewen, and even with her dark thoughts, couldn't help but give an inward smile. He really did look like James Bond trying desperately to be a cowboy in his starched jeans and pressed Western shirt.

She couldn't allow herself to read too much into his few touches or kisses. He was here to find out why she was in Scotland, and that was the end of it. He didn't trust her, and she was pretty sure he was holding out on her. She hadn't forgotten his computer skills on the plane. Skills that very few people possessed.

Turning into the driveway, she finally allowed herself to consider her grandparents as suspects. Could what Ewen said be true? Did they want custody of Riley badly enough to destroy Tempe and the ranch? She remembered Riley's excited phone call about showing Gamy and PawPaw around the ranch. The thought made Tempe bring the truck to a screeching halt in front of the house.

The mere idea of the older couple trying to ingratiate themselves into Riley's life for ulterior motives infuriated her. She flung the creaky truck door open and moved toward the house. She was halfway there when a strong hand grabbed her arm and spun her around.

"What?" she said forcefully as she faced Ewen.

His calm veneer had the opposite effect on her, and she jerked her arm out of his grasp.

"Tempe, listen, I only made the suggestion about your grandparents to consider all angles. That doesn't mean I'm right. They said someone contacted them about the happenings on the ranch. Let's find out who before we jump to any conclusions."

Tempe closed her eyes and took a deep breath. He was right. She knew it, but she wanted to protect Riley from any hurt. She opened her eyes and stared at Ewen. "You don't have any children?" The media had never reported a marriage for their favorite famous author and Bachelor of the Year, but that didn't mean he didn't have children.

"No."

"Well, until you do, and understand where I'm coming from, stay out of my way."

Her words were harsh, and she regretted the hurt that flashed in his eyes, but her main concern was her daughter. Until someone had children, there was no way they could understand the protective instincts that flared to life when something or someone threatened that child's happiness.

She turned back toward the house, but his words had hit home. She wouldn't deny Riley the chance to get to know her gamy and pawpaw, but they better be on the up and up, or they'd have Tempe to deal with.

As she approached the house, she was glad to see one of Ned's men show himself, nod at her and then disappear. She did appreciate Ewen providing security. She could never have afforded it.

As soon as she hit the top step of the porch, the screen door flew open and Riley catapulted into her arms, babbling a mile a minute.

"Mama, Ewen called and said you passed your test." Surprised and pleased at that piece of news, Tempe glanced over her shoulder at Ewen. He grinned and shrugged.

"I'm so glad you get to finish flying with the

Angels." Right after Riley said that, a haggard-looking Minerva and Franklin slowly came up behind Tempe's daughter.

"I've been showing Gamy and PawPaw the ranch. Those men stayed with us everywhere we went, so we were safe. I tried to get Gamy on a horse, but she didn't wanna ride, but PawPaw gave it a shot. He did real good, too. He only fell off once."

Tempe studied the older couple more closely. Minerva's hair hung in silver hanks around her head, and if Tempe wasn't mistaken, she had on some of Effie's old clothes—jeans, a worn blouse and a pair of old boots. She certainly didn't look anything like the haughty woman Tempe had left at the ranch. And Franklin just looked frazzled.

Wiping her hands on a dish towel, Effie stuck her head out of the kitchen and into the hall. "We're having an early lunch." She looked at Tempe and nodded. "A celebratory lunch. Ewen called to let us know you passed your evaluation." Her voice became firm. "He also explained what happened on the way to Florida."

Minerva's head snapped up and she straightened her posture, going for the haughty look but not quite managing it, what with her dusty clothes and unkempt hair.

"No one has seen fit to tell *me* what happened." Tempe opened her mouth to tell Minerva it wasn't any of her business, but Ewen stepped in front of her, effectively cutting her off, both physically and verbally.

"Minerva, Franklin" he crooned, "let's get settled at the table for lunch." He swiveled his head in Riley's direction. "Riley, why don't you go wash your hands."

Riley turned her big green eyes toward him, and Tempe crossed her arms over her chest. It was going to be interesting to see how Ewen handled her intelligent and very inquisitive daughter.

"Mr. Ewen, I know you wanna talk where I can't hear, but I'll just leave and sneak back so's I can hear what y'all are saying, so's you might as well let me stay."

Ewen looked at Tempe over his shoulder and she shrugged. If he was planning on staying at the ranch for any length of time, he might as well learn how to deal with Tempe's precocious daughter.

He turned back to Riley. "Riley, you're right. The adults need to discuss some things and we'd appreciate it if you'd give us a few minutes while you go clean up for lunch." He raised a very James Bond brow. "And if you promise not to eavesdrop, I have a very important job for you later."

Tempe's little negotiator crossed her arms over her chest, much like Tempe herself. "What kind of job?"

Ewen's brow raised a tad higher and Tempe wanted to laugh.

"You'll find out later, if you abide by the terms of our agreement."

Riley studied him a moment, nodded, then turned to Tempe. "Mama, I know you're worried Gamy and PawPaw want to take me away from you 'cause of the things happening around the ranch, but I want 'em to stay here 'cause they're the only family we have left 'sides Aunt Effie and Aunt Liv. I know they've changed their minds 'cause they can see how good you take care of me. They'd never take me away from here 'cause they love me and I love them and they know you need me." She shifted toward Minerva and Franklin. "Ain't that right, Gamy?"

Tempe almost choked when Minerva's mouth flopped open and closed like a fish. If Tempe still believed in God, she'd say He had a sense of humor, using a child to put them all in their place.

But that didn't negate the fact that Tempe had a lot of questions for her grandparents, so she stepped in to handle her daughter. "Riley, time to wash up, and give us ten minutes until you come down to lunch."

Riley nodded and her dirty-blond ponytail, a duplicate of Tempe's, flopped up and down. "Yes'm," she said, and fled up the stairs.

Before Ewen had a chance to intervene and

play the peacemaker, Tempe looked directly at Minerva. She wanted answers and she wanted them now.

"I have one question. Are you trying to kill me in order to gain custody of my daughter?"

Ewen closed his eyes in frustration. He couldn't believe Tempe had so boldly asked that question. He could almost feel the temperature dropping as Minerva steeled her spine and shot visual daggers at Tempe.

"How dare you ask that question."

Tempe strode forward and got in her face. "I dare because you showed up here right in the middle of this mess, demanding custody of my daughter, and you have the resources to make it all happen. Ewen and I could have been killed in that plane yesterday when those guys tried to shoot us down."

Minerva paled and swayed forward. Ewen moved to take her by the elbow and led her to the kitchen where he seated her in a chair at the table. With a vein-riddled, shaky hand, Minerva rubbed her temple.

"How can you even say such a thing?"

Tempe sat down across from the older lady and both men took a seat. Effie placed a glass of water in front of Minerva, a look of pity lining her face. Dudley stood quietly, facing the sink.

Tempe leaned forward on her elbows. Her tone softened a bit, but she was still firm. Ewen decided to stay quiet. It was time for Tempe and her grandmother to talk and, hopefully, heal years of bitterness and anger. He prayed that would happen.

"Minerva, you mentioned someone contacted you and said Riley's life was in danger. I need the name of that person."

Minerva raised her head and looked as if she'd aged years in a matter of minutes. "I would never harm any of you. I—I was scared of losing our only great-granddaughter. The only one left who m-might be able to forgive an old woman's foolishness." Tears pooled in her eyes. "We lost our daughter years ago, and before we had a chance to make it right, she was lost to me forever. You were already seventeen and Olivia was nineteen when my Sara and your father, Ben, died in that plane crash, and now you're telling me you could have died in a plane crash, too." Franklin nodded sadly, agreeing with his wife.

Resignation filled her voice. "I called after Sara and Ben died, and Olivia was very angry. I knew then we'd never have a second chance with the two of you. We had allowed too much time to pass." She swallowed back a sob. "When we got the note saying Riley's life was in jeopardy, we came here as fast as we could. The only way we knew to keep her safe was to threaten to sue for custody because we both knew you and Olivia hated us for turning our backs on your mother all those years ago."

The kitchen went deathly quiet. Ewen noticed tears in Effie's eyes as she stood completely still, with a spatula gripped tightly in her hand. A single tear rolled down Minerva's face and Franklin's expression was one of resignation. Ewen glanced at Tempe and the only movement he spotted was a tic beneath her right eye.

"Olivia never told me you called." It was almost a whisper. Ewen wanted nothing more than to wrap Tempe in his arms to comfort her, but he stayed seated.

The tears were now flowing freely down Minerva's face. "I—I know you'll never be able to forgive us. It was foolish of us to think your father wasn't good enough for our daughter. It really wasn't pride, you see, we later realized no man would be good enough for her because we didn't want to let go of our only child and have her live all the way across the country."

Tempe squirmed in her seat and Ewen could only imagine the riot of emotions churning in her heart and mind. He said another quick prayer for healing. Ewen wouldn't be the man he was today without his ornery grandfather constantly interfering in his life.

"Tempe, do you think you and Olivia could give us another chance to make things right?" the all-too-quiet Franklin whispered.

Tempe leaned forward on her elbows and forced a smile. "It looks like my daughter has already made that choice for me, but—" she raised her chin "—I don't want to hear another word about suing for custody, and I want the name of the person who contacted you."

Minerva gave a weak smile and nodded her agreement. "Thank you," she whispered, then cleared her throat. "We received a note in the mail. There was no return address, and no signature, but it was postmarked Texas. I assume it came from someone in this area. And Tempe, please believe me when I say we haven't been involved in anything happening to you or the ranch. We received the note and came straight here."

Tempe rolled her shoulders back and stared at Minerva for the longest time. "Okay, you're welcome to stay for a while, and we'll see how it goes." Tempe jabbed her thumb at Ewen. "He's gonna help me find out who's doing all this, and we'll soon put a stop to it."

Shocking Ewen, Minerva turned her full haughtiness on him. "I want to know exactly why a famous fictional novelist is in Texas, of all places, bothering my granddaughter."

Tempe moaned and dropped her face into her

hands. Then she did the most amazing thing. She raised her head and grinned at him, a challenge lighting her eyes, as if to say, "You started this, so you handle it." His heart skipped a beat at her radiant beauty and took a moment to settle back into place.

"I, um—"

Minerva rolled her eyes, which definitely didn't go with her sophisticated personality, and waved a hand in the air. "Forget I asked. That's the same look Ben had in his eyes when he looked at my Sara, and we all know how that turned out."

Startled, Tempe straightened in her chair and Ewen tried to explain.

"No, it's not—"

"You don't understand—"

They both spoke at the same time, and stopped simultaneously.

Minerva took control of the situation. Ewen cringed when she lifted her chin and assumed her proud look. "I'll say this, if anyone dares to harm a hair on the head of our grandchildren or our great-grandchild, they'll have to deal with me."

Tempe's surprised expression at the vehemence in Minerva's voice was priceless. Ewen sighed in relief. Things would work out. They always did when God became involved.

Riley's voice preceded her appearance at the kitchen doorway, making everyone relax.

Small hands propped on her hips—reminding Ewen so much of her mother—Riley said, "I hope y'all got everything worked out, because I'm hungry. I didn't listen in—" her gaze zeroed in on Ewen "—so's I get my surprise job." Her hands fell from her nonexistent hips and she moved to Tempe's side.

"You gonna let Gamy and PawPaw stay, Mama?"

Tempe folded Riley in her arms and Ewen's heart melted just a little bit more, but he shored up the unwanted feelings that he couldn't allow.

"Yes, Riley, everyone is going to stay, but," she said, letting the last word hang in the air, "everyone has to follow the rules and have one of Ned's men with them if they leave the house. We're going to catch whoever's doing all this, but until then, I want everyone safe."

Everyone in the room nodded their agreement, and Riley, apparently satisfied that the adults had behaved, turned her attention back on Ewen with an intensity only an eight-year-old could achieve.

"What's my surprise job?"

"Riley," Tempe chided, "that's rude. We can wait until after lunch."

Ewen held up a hand. "No, she abided by the conditions of the agreement and deserves to know her surprise job." Truth be told, Ewen was enjoying himself. Maybe a little too much, considering the situation. He'd never been around a family as relaxed and comfortable in their own skins as Tempe and Riley were.

"Riley, your mother showed me the map that may lead to gold and I came to some very interesting conclusions."

Minerva gasped and stared at Tempe. "The map and gold you mentioned earlier? It's actually real? I know you said you didn't want to lose Riley's home, but you're trying to locate gold to save the ranch?" Minerva slapped a hand on the table, startling everyone in the room. "I won't have it. Tempe, if you need money to save this ranch, you'll get it from me. I have more than all of us could spend in a lifetime."

Stunned silence filled the room once again until Tempe stirred. Ewen wasn't quite sure how to read her expression, because her face had gone blank.

"Minerva, I appreciate the offer, but we can handle this."

Minerva looked a little crestfallen, but rallied quickly. "Then I'll help you find this gold," she said, determination filling every word.

Riley shifted on her feet. "What'd ya find out about the map? Mama and I have hunted and hunted for the gold and we can't find it."

Ewen focused on Riley and he prayed there

was actually gold to be found. "I studied the map, and I believe it's a tableau map—"

Tempe cleared her throat and Ewen got the message. "Without going into details, I believe there has to be another map to lay beneath the one your mother showed me. When you place it under the map we have, it'll show the entire topography, uh, picture, not just part of it."

Riley scrunched up her nose and it was the cutest thing Ewen had ever seen. "In other words, my surprise job is to help us find the second map?"

He nodded in the affirmative.

Riley stood there a moment, chewing on her lower lip, then a wide grin split her face. "Well, it's a good thing you gave me this job, because I know exactly where the other map is."

FIFTEEN

The room exploded in conversation after Riley's big announcement, and Tempe gaped at her daughter. "Riley, why didn't you tell me about this other map?"

Riley shifted from foot to foot and glanced apologetically toward Franklin Roderick. "Paw-Paw, I had to call you that 'cause I called Great-Grampie Grampie. Anyways, a little ways before he passed on, Grampie came to my room one night and said he had a bedtime story for me. He was always telling good stories about the Wild West."

Tempe's eyes widened when Ewen's castle cat, Simba, came strolling disdainfully into the kitchen and hopped right into Minerva's lap. Even though she said she was allergic, the older woman automatically smoothed a hand down the cat's back and the male tabby purred loudly. Her attention was drawn back to Riley when she spoke.

She'd have to think about the change in Minerva later.

"Grampie told me a story about him finding the gold, and he drew me a map showing me where it was." She looked at Tempe. "Mama, Grampie told me it was a special secret between me and him and that he'd tell you when the time was right. It was real exciting. He told me to keep the map in a safe place in my room, and when you got the map after Grampie died, I figured it was the same one."

Tempe's heart was beating faster than it did when performing a chair-flying stunt with the Angels. "Riley, where's the map Grampie drew you?"

A wide grin spread across Riley's face. "I thought real hard about where to hide it, and I found the perfect place."

Tempe concentrated on slowing her heart rate down. Could it possibly be this easy? Nothing in her life had ever been easy. She smiled at her daughter, who was so much more important than gold. "And where is that, sweetheart?"

"In my Bible, of course. If a bad man wants to steal something, I don't think he's gonna go looking in a Bible. That map goes to church with me and Aunt Effie every Sunday."

Ewen cleared his throat, and Tempe ignored

him, but something in her hardened heart shifted and opened a little.

"Can you go get it for us?"

"Yes, ma'am!" Riley said, excitement trembling in her voice.

When she rushed out of the room, it felt to Tempe as if a whirlwind had come and gone. She loved her daughter so much it made her heart hurt. Her gaze drifted toward Ewen and his smile contained knowledge and understanding. From the beginning, he had promoted a healing of her family. Her gaze trekked across the table to Minerva, who in such a short amount of time had made such a big change. She sat there with the large tabby filling her lap, sneezed once, and stared at Tempe.

"Tempe, I mean it, Franklin and I want to be a part of this family. We'll help you find your gold, and—" her lower lip trembled until she lifted that stubborn chin "—we're going to help you win this fight. Every resource we have is at your disposal. Even though you won't take any money, we want you to know that you and Olivia and Riley will inherit everything we own. Might as well put it to good use now."

For the first time in her life, Tempe didn't know how to respond. She was so used to fighting every battle on her own, and now she had Minerva, Franklin, Liv and Ewen standing at her side. Of course, Ewen still had his own agenda, but his brother had brought in security and that meant a lot. Maybe not enough for her to tell him her secrets. She couldn't risk him claiming the gold for himself because the map was in a book sold to his grandfather. And as much as she appreciated Minerva's offer, it was still too soon in their new relationship to take her up on her offer of financial assistance.

Riley came barreling into the room with Kylo on her heels, saving Tempe from having to respond to something that would take time for her to assess. It shocked her even further when Minerva gave Kylo a stern look and firmly said, "Kylo, sit!" Even more amazing, the dog did as she asked. Minerva picked up a scrap off the table and presented it as a reward.

Had the whole world changed overnight? Tempe shook off the odd happenings and focused on the piece of paper in Riley's hand. "May I see it?"

Riley handed it over and everyone leaned across the table when she laid it down and smoothed it out with her hand. She could actually feel Ewen's breath on her neck as he peered over her shoulder. It brought back memories of their kiss, but she forced herself to concentrate on the map. Ewen turned and grabbed the clear map he'd had made in Florida off the kitchen countertop.

Nudging her to the side, he laid it over Riley's map, and there it was. Tempe knew exactly where the gold was. Everyone reacted at her sharp intake of breath, but Ewen was the first to speak.

"You know where it is." It wasn't a question, but a quiet statement of fact.

Could it be true? Was there really gold? Well, there was only one way to find out. "Yes, I know exactly where it is. It's hidden in a cave in one of the larger foothills on our property, the hills before you get to the mountains."

Everyone started talking at once, eager to go treasure hunting, but Tempe held up a hand, effectively quieting the room. "I know everyone is excited, but we have to be careful. Someone has been systematically destroying this ranch, among other things." She didn't talk about the attempts on her life in front of Riley. "I don't know if it has anything to do with the map and the gold, but if it does, we don't want to lead anyone to the hiding place, and we don't want to take unnecessary risks."

Everyone nodded begrudgingly, their enthusiasm dampened, so Tempe added, "What we need is a plan."

That simple statement got everyone riled up again and she and Ewen shared a silent grin. It hit her like a ton of bricks—she hadn't had anyone to share private moments with since Riley was born, and it felt... Well, it felt good. She'd have to think about that later.

Everyone was talking over each other, figuring out a way to safely get the gold, when Tempe heard a low growl underlying all the talk. She glanced at Kylo. He was standing, the fur on the back of his neck raised. She followed his line of vision and looked at the door leading outside from the kitchen. Before she even had a chance to check out the situation, the door slammed open and John, one of Ned's men staggered through, holding his left arm, blood pulsing out from under his fingers.

"Get everyone to a safe place. Now!"

Tempe took immediate control of the situation. She'd been trained for battle and it came naturally. She questioned the man with the bleeding arm. "Sniper or close in?"

"Sniper," he said.

"Are the rest of the men okay?"

He nodded and handed her his earwig. "Here, you can reconnaissance with them."

Tempe took the communication device and placed it in her ear, but first she had to secure her family. And oddly enough, Minerva and Franklin were now a part of that group. She couldn't imagine what Liv would say when Tempe apprised her of these new developments.

"Effie," she barked out, "take everyone to the back of the house and see to John's wounds. Y'all stay put until I get back."

She turned and bumped into Ewen. "I'm coming with you," he said.

She shook her head. "Listen, Ewen, this is my fight. I appreciate the offer, but I don't think a famous writer, or Bachelor of the Year, getting hurt or killed on my ranch would be a good idea." Plus, from a personal standpoint, she didn't like the idea of him getting hurt—a fact she wasn't inclined to look at too closely.

"I'm coming with or without your permission."

Determination filled his voice and she didn't have time to argue. She'd had enough of someone threatening her family and it was time to put a stop to it.

"Fine." If he wanted to risk his neck, that was his choice. He was a big boy. Everyone had disappeared from the kitchen. She headed for the coat closet in the hallway and pulled open the door. Shoving clothing out of the way, she reached into the back and pulled out two rifles. Turning, she tossed one to Ewen and handed him a round of ammunition.

"They're semiautomatic AR 15s, but they'll get the job done. If it's a sniper, he might be long gone, but it's time to go on the offense. I'm finished playing defense."

Ewen loaded the weapon like an expert and she raised a brow. "You and I are going to have long, serious talk real soon. Let's go."

Weapons up, Ewen and Tempe scanned the area for danger as they moved toward the old truck. They both got in and he wrangled his door shut. She might be used to handling things herself, but he refused to allow her to risk her life alone. He spent most of his time with the DIA working on a computer, but that didn't mean he wasn't fully trained, and he'd always had good instincts.

His attention was snagged when she turned the key to power the engine and it turned over but didn't catch. She began to try again, but something clicked in his mind about the sound it made.

"Tempe, stop," he said quietly, trying to figure it out. She stilled her hand and he quickly went over the past twenty minutes in his mind, assessing the information. Why would a sniper want to remove one of the guards, but do nothing else? Why such a targeted move, and then it hit him.

"Tempe, get out of the truck quickly. Whatever you do, *do not* start the ignition."

Her head snapped toward him. "Bomb?"

"Out of the truck now!" he said, fighting with

the rusted door before finally flinging it open. His gut was screaming he was right. He ran around the truck, ready to help Tempe back to the house, but she was still sitting in the driver's seat, struggling with the door.

Ewen grabbed the outside handle and pulled as hard as he could, but it was stuck. Placing a booted foot against the side of the truck, he pulled with every ounce of strength he had and finally, finally it gave. He almost fell when it swung open, but he steadied himself and grabbed Tempe by the arm, pulling her out.

They got their bearings and ran as hard as they could, but not hard enough. His feet lifted from the ground, and he was airborne as an explosion rent the air. He hit the gravel driveway on his side, but fell forward onto his stomach. Tempe!

He lifted his head and frantically searched the area closest to him. His heart pounding in his chest and his eyes watering from the smoke, he pushed himself to his knees. The smoke finally cleared enough for him to see Tempe crumpled on the ground. He got up and stumbled toward her. His hand shaking, he placed two fingers on her neck, checking for a pulse. When he felt a strong heartbeat, he closed his eyes and thanked the Good Lord for sparing her life.

She rolled over onto her back before he could force her to stop and those sharp, green eyes blinked open. There was his warrior, in all her fighting splendor.

"I'm gonna put a stop to this mess. We need a plan."

He couldn't help but grin at her tenacity. "Well, you've come to the right man. I'm quite brilliant at planning strategies."

She narrowed her eyes but allowed him to help her up. They stood there a moment, staring at the burning remains of the rusted-out old truck.

"How did you figure it out?" she asked.

"When you turned the key, and the engine didn't catch the first time, something didn't feel right. I assessed everything that had happened and had to ask myself why a sharpshooter would injure only one member of the security detail, then it hit me. They removed the guy closest to the house so they could plant the bomb."

Her face covered in soot, she narrowed her eyes again. "For a fiction writer, you sure do know a lot."

He rubbed a hand down his face and it came away with grime. "Yes, well, I do try." This wasn't the time to tell her about his work with the DIA. He was only beginning to gain her trust, and after the betrayals she'd lived through with Riley's father, and the history with her grandparents, she'd feel betrayed once again if he told her the truth.

Before he could say anything else, two things happened simultaneously. The front door to the house opened, Tempe's whole family, and Dudley, spilling out, and two vehicles came tearing down the driveway.

He tensed until he recognized the man driving the jeep. The driver of the car was a woman with a frantic look on her face. To be on the safe side, Ewen scoured the ground and spotted his AR 15. Whipping it into his hands, he kept the weapon lowered at his side, just in case. He was surprised when Tempe spoke.

"Liv? What's she doing here?"

"That's your sister?"

Tempe nodded, her lips firm. "And that's Ned in the Jeep," he said.

She turned to him. "Why are my sister and your brother here?"

He directed his gaze to the man and woman shooting each other suspicious glances when they exited their vehicles.

"We'll have to ask them."

The whole family converged on them at the same time that Ned and Liv approached the group.

"What happened?"

"Is anyone hurt?"

"Was that a bomb?"

"We heard a big noise and came running."

Ewen held up a hand and everyone quieted. His heart melted when Riley sidled up to her mother and held on tight. No eight-year-old should have to experience what was happening at the ranch. It was time, as Tempe had said, to put a stop to it.

His eyes met Ned's and his brother gave a curt nod. Ewen wasn't surprised to see him. He knew Ned's men would report everything happening at the ranch.

He addressed everyone standing there with a million questions on their lips. "The most important thing is that no one was hurt. The second most important thing is we need to take this inside. I'm sure whoever was here is gone, but it's only prudent to take all precautions."

Tempe poked him in the side. "You do have a funny way with words."

He grinned, happy to see her joking in the middle of this mess. She was unlike any other woman he knew. Spunky to the core.

Before he could herd them inside, Minerva pointed a finger at Ned. "I refuse to go anywhere until you explain who that large man is."

Ewen winced. Ned's new wife referred to Ned as Mountain Man, and the description did fit nicely. "That's my brother. He's here to help."

Minerva scrutinized him a moment, then nodded. "Okay, he can come inside."

Ewen smiled at the way Minerva had taken

over protecting her family, but not everyone was happy. Tempe's sister, Liv, appeared at Tempe's side as the group walked toward the house, and Ewen caught wisps of the conversation.

"I want to know what's been going on around here, and I demand to know how Minerva and Franklin Roderick ended up on our property. Our grandparents turned their backs on our mother and haven't seen fit to contact us since the funeral."

They moved out of hearing range and Ned chuckled in Ewen's left ear. For such a large man, he moved like a panther, quiet and deadly. "Looks like you have your hands full, bruv. Woman trouble?"

There was a wealth of inquiry in that one question. Ned was a man of few words, but now wasn't the time. "It's complicated. We'll talk later."

Ned gave a curt nod and Ewen knew it was time to come clean with his family about his clandestine life. As far as Tempe and woman trouble, well, that area of his life was a bit murky at the moment. He had suspicions, but he ached for her to tell him the truth on her own volition. That would be a perfect time for him to share his secrets with her. A natural trade-off.

Ewen and Ned brought up the rear, and when they stepped into the kitchen and heard raised voices, Ned made the understatement of the year. "Bruv, I believe you've landed yourself right in the middle of a hornet's nest."

SIXTEEN

Tempe closed her eyes against the frustration building inside her. She should have kept Liv updated on the situation, but it was all she could do to keep the ranch running, get her Blue Angels psych eval over with, fight an unseen enemy and keep everyone safe.

She opened her eyes and mouth at the same time. "Quiet," she yelled. Dead silence met her exclamation and she looked at every person in the room. Her family, such as it was. Liv was red-faced mad, Minerva practically stomping her "new" old boots on the floor with Franklin by her side, Kylo was spinning, chasing his tail due to the tension in the room, and Simba sat in the corner, ignoring everyone, grooming himself. Riley stood close to Minerva in what looked like a protective mode against Liv's tongue-lashing. Dudley stood off to the side.

"Riley, the adults need to talk. I'd appreciate it if you'd go to your room and stay there." Riley nodded seriously and left the room. "Minerva, Franklin, Dudley, Ned and Aunt Effie, take a seat," Tempe ordered. The older ones in the room sat and all eyes were trained on Tempe. Could Ewen be right? Could their family be healed, regardless of the baggage they carried? If she still believed in God, this would be a good time to ask for help, but she'd handled everything on her own for so long she didn't know what to ask, or if she even wanted to.

"I know all of you have a lot of questions," she gave Liv a hard stare when her talkative sister's lips parted. "And we'll get to that later. Right now, we're going to focus on the danger someone has brought to this family, and figure out a way to stop it."

She brought everyone, mainly Liv and Ned, up to date on all the events and happenings on the ranch, as well as the attack on the Cessna when she and Ewen traveled to Florida. Ned's eyes narrowed dangerously at that piece of information, and he sliced a hard look at Ewen.

When she finished, she held up her hand against any questions bubbling forth and asked Ewen to give them his thoughts and possible culprits. He'd offered to help her, and she was taking him up on it. As he moved to her side, they shared another one of those unspoken private looks that made her a little uncomfortable. She didn't know exactly what was going on between them, but she did know they both had secrets, and that didn't work in any kind of relationship. Not even friendship. Although, she had to admit, she admired the way he took command of the room.

"The first thing we have to ascertain is whether there's one or multiple factions causing the problems."

Tempe cleared her throat. "Plain English, please."

He grinned and Tempe felt the tension in the room lessen as everyone riveted their eyes back and forth between Tempe and Ewen.

He started again, "As I said, we have to find out whether one person is causing all the trouble, or if it's two different people and two different situations." He held up a finger. "One, we know Thomas Hildebrand offered to buy the ranch from Tempe's grandfather several months before he died, then a second offer was made to Tempe after he died."

He held up a second finger. "Two, one incident happened in the air on the way to Florida and that possibly indicates a different person or group. I understand a few people aren't happy to have a female Blue Angel in their squad." He held up a third finger. "And three, we can't discount the possibility that someone outside of the family knows about the gold. The probability that all current events are related is around seventy-five percent."

Tempe noticed the sharp look that Ned sent Ewen, but Minerva spoke first.

"And how did you come to that conclusion, young man?"

All eyes turned to Ewen, and Tempe grinned at the uncomfortable expression on his face. "Well, um, I'm good at assessing probabilities based on the gathering of factual information presented in a timely manner."

Blank faces met his explanation and he cleared his throat. "Let's just say, based on the information, that's my best guess."

"So where do we start?" The quiet question came from Effie, and Tempe studied her aunt. She thought it interesting when Dudley slipped his arm around Aunt Effie in a comforting matter. A wave of guilt came over Tempe. She'd taken her aunt for granted. Effie had always been there for Tempe and Riley, never carving out a life of her own. Could it be that Effie and Dudley were attracted to each other? If they were, Tempe vowed to support Effie in whatever made her happy.

Ewen looked pointedly at Tempe, and she liked that he asked her before taking over. It showed he was a team player, and he didn't think that just because he was a man, he should run the show.

Because of that, she waved a hand in his general direction.

"You've done good so far. What's our next step?"

He smiled and looked at the whole group. "First, I think Tempe and I should pay a visit to Thomas Hildebrand and do a frontal assault to gauge his reaction."

Everyone nodded their agreement, and Effie spoke again. "Before that, we're going to eat lunch. It's almost two o'clock now, and I think visiting Thomas can wait until tomorrow morning, after everyone has settled from the day's events."

Tempe agreed with her aunt. "Sounds good."

Riley was invited back down and lunch was a noisy affair, with everyone speculating about the gold and who might be responsible for the destruction of their property. With Riley at the table, no one mentioned the attempts on Tempe's life, and she was grateful for that. As soon as the table was cleared, Liv grabbed Tempe by the arm, dragged her up the stairs, pushed Tempe into her own bedroom and slammed the door shut behind them. Turning on her, Liv released a torrent of questions without pausing for air.

Tempe held up a hand for silence and her sister piped down.

"One question at a time, please." And of

course, her brilliant attorney sister targeted the area Tempe least wanted to discuss.

"I ran a light background check on Ewen Duncan after we talked, and I want to know what a famous fictional novelist, whose family lives in a huge castle in Scotland, is doing on our ranch in the middle of nowhere?"

Tempe patted a place beside her on the bed and Liv slowly crossed the room and sat down.

"It's a long story."

Liv glanced away. "I've got plenty of time."

Tempe poked a finger on her sister's thigh. "Tit for tat, sis, but we'll deal with your problems later." Tempe took a deep breath and began. "You know about the map Granddad left us?"

"Tempe, you can't believe that map is real. I know Ewen mentioned it, but a treasure map? Gold? Why didn't Granddad retrieve it when he was alive?"

"That's a question I've asked myself a thousand times, but the thing is, Liv…" Tempe really didn't want to go into this right now, but she had no choice. "I've told you the ranch has been operating on a shoestring budget for several years now, and if we don't get a good price on the beef cattle this year, we might go bust. I can only assume Granddad found out about the gold right before he died."

Liv took in a sharp breath, but Tempe kept

going before she could fire out more questions. "In the letter that accompanied his will, he was so adamant about the map and the gold, and several weeks after the funeral, I decided to check into it. It turns out that in order to help raise money to pay the bills, Effie sold several valuable books, not realizing Granddad had hidden a map inside one of them.

"She sold it to a bookstore here in Texas and Ewen's grandfather called the store and bought it. I went to Scotland and found the book and the map, but I didn't know they had security cameras in the room and Ewen saw me take something from the book and slip it into my pocket." She let out a huff of breath. "That's why he's here. To find out what I took from the library in the castle." She gave Liv a sharp look. "Not for any other reason. I haven't told him why I was in Scotland because he might have grounds to claim the map and the gold, since they bought the book fair and square. I don't know what the legality is in a case like this. Maybe you have a better idea."

Liv nodded. "I'll check into it." Studying her fingernails, she shot out another question, just like a whip-smart attorney and annoying older sister would do. "Then how did that picture of you being kissed in the cockpit of your plane come about?"

Tempe didn't know how to respond, because

her feelings were a mass of confusion when it came to Ewen. "It didn't mean anything. It just happened."

"Who kissed whom?"

"What?"

"It's a simple question. Did you kiss him, or did he kiss you?"

Tempe snarled. "What does that have to do with anything?"

Liv smacked her sister on the shoulder. "It makes all the difference in the world. You never were the romantic type. Give you a horse and an airplane or helicopter and you're happy." Liv turned serious. "Tempe, it's been a long time since Riley was born. As far as I know, you haven't even dated, although I know you've been asked out. Promise me, if you find yourself falling for Ewen, you'll give the man a chance. Promise me."

Could she do that? Could she ever trust another man after Riley's father left without a backward glance? Knowing Liv was waiting for an answer, she shrugged, trying to lighten the mood. "I'll do my best. Does that satisfy you?"

Giving Tempe a knowing smirk, Liv moved on to the next uncomfortable subject. "How in the world did our estranged grandparents end up here? I couldn't believe my eyes when I drove up and saw them. I recognized them because they attended our parents' funeral and they're in the New York society pages quite often, attending charities and such. I live in New York and they never attempted to contact me."

Tempe shook her head. "Maybe they never contacted you because you gave them the cold shoulder when they called after our parents died—something, by the way, you failed to mention to me."

Liv puffed up like a fearful dog. "It wasn't worth mentioning. I told them if our parents weren't good enough for them to visit when they were alive, they certainly weren't invited to the funeral, but they came anyway."

"Harsh words, Liv."

"Tempe, they disowned our mother when she married Dad. They didn't deserve consideration."

"Well, they're here now, and because of Riley, I think they're turning over a new leaf. They want to be part of the family."

Tempe decided it best not to mention the custody threat. Liv would flip out.

"Minerva does look different," Liv contemplated, then grinned. "I'm sure Riley showed them all over the ranch. Please tell me she got them on a horse."

Tempe's lips curved and Liv laughed.

"I love it!"

"Promise me you'll give them a chance because of Riley, if for no other reason."

"Okay, but if either Minerva or Franklin crosses me, I'm letting them have it, and I'm never calling her Grandmother or him Grandfather."

"Fair enough."

Two heavy treads passed their room, moving down the hall, and Liv made Tempe laugh when she said, "Looks like the boys are having a gab session same as us girls."

Ewen followed Ned into his bedroom and closed the door behind them. For a man of few words, Ned became quite chatty.

"So you follow a woman to Texas because she stole something from the castle library, then you kiss her in the cockpit of a plane she's flying? These women of ours tend to sneak up on us that way."

Ewen's head snapped up. "You already knew what happened to us in the plane on the way to Florida?"

"I know a lot of things, bruv."

"Ned, this isn't the same circumstance as what happened between you and Mary Grace. I don't think this will have the same happy ending."

"Why not?" his blunt brother asked.

Ewen heaved a heavy sigh. "She hasn't told me

what she took in Scotland. And well, there's quite a few things she doesn't know about me. And added to that, we live in two different countries."

Ned stared him down. "We'll get to your secrets in a minute. Do you have feelings for this woman?"

The sweet kiss they shared flowed through his mind, but he shook his head. "It's impossible. There's too much standing between us, and she's been badly hurt in the past."

"And if there was nothing standing between you?"

Ewen didn't want to talk about that right now because he didn't know the answer. It was time to come clean about his position with the DIA, but before he had a chance, his brother surprised him again.

"I can see you aren't ready to talk about your relationship with Ms. Calloway, so why don't you tell me about your work with the DIA."

"You've been out of the CIA since before you met Mary Grace. How did you find out about my position with the Defense Intelligence Agency?"

"How do you think?"

Ewen shook his head. Judging by Ned's grin, he was afraid he knew the answer. "Don't tell me you found out from Alfred?"

Ned grinned wider and nodded in the affirmative.

"How does a butler who lives in a castle in Scotland get that kind of information?"

"It's my opinion that our grandfather and old Alfred know more than we do. Maybe they have a secret or two themselves. But I'm proud of you, bruv. The United States has been good to our family, and we owe our mother's birthplace our allegiance. You're in a good position to be of great help to them."

Ewen sighed. "I should have told you sooner, but you've always been overly protective of everyone in the family, and you had major problems of your own."

"I'm here to help, if you need me. I'll stay in the background and help protect if that's what you want, but I'm not leaving until I'm sure you're safe. You're my brother and I've a right to see to your health. You do intelligence work with the DIA, but you're not in the field very much the way I was with the CIA."

"I appreciate that. As I told everyone in the kitchen, I think we should start by having a chat with Thomas Hildebrand in person so I can gauge his reaction to our questions."

"Sounds like a plan," Ned said, moving silently across the room and stopping at the door. "I checked on Thomas Hildebrand and the sheriff, as you asked me to. On the surface, they come up clean, but I'll probe deeper. I'll be outside with the boys, and we'll take care of John, but I'll be shadowing you in case you need me."

Ewen swallowed hard. Ned had left his new wife to come help him, and the words he wanted to say clogged in his throat, but Ned handled the emotional situation.

"I luv ye, too, bruv. Stay safe. Me and the men will be around as long as ye need us."

For such a large man, his exit was unnaturally silent. The door closed with a whisper and Ewen sat on the side of his bed. He thought about the danger circling Tempe and her family. Anger filled him at the thought of Riley possibly getting hurt, and the filthy hands of the kidnappers who had dared to touch the child. That, as much as anything, gave him the resolve to help Tempe figure out exactly where the danger was coming from.

Which reminded him… He stood and retrieved his laptop, did a quick search, then made a deal that cost quite a bit of money due to time restraints. Pulling his suitcase out of the closet, he opened a hidden compartment and withdrew a small device that would track Riley the world over. After a moment's hesitation, he pulled out a second device and grinned, thinking of Tempe's reaction if she knew he was going to be able to track her every movement.

SEVENTEEN

The next morning, after a chaotic breakfast with her family, Tempe was ready to escape, but she had a small chat with Liv before leaving, making her promise to play nice with the grandparents. Based on her sister's mulish expression, she didn't think her request was very effective. She loved her sister, but Liv had always been hardheaded. Brilliantly smart, but extremely stubborn.

Ewen was waiting on her at the front door and Tempe whistled for Kylo to join them. The young, energetic dog barreled from the kitchen into the foyer, coming to a dead stop in front of her.

"Good boy," she praised.

Ewen lifted a brow and it annoyed her. Kylo was still in training and he was young. "What?"

"We're taking the dog with us to see Thomas Hildebrand?"

"You got a problem with that?"

"No, but you may want to restrain him from biting someone in the behind."

Tempe pushed past him and Kylo trotted after her when she gave him a release cue, but she nearly stumbled in shock when she got out the door. "What. Is. That?"

"It's a new dually truck with four-wheel drive. I researched trucks yesterday evening and this one seems appropriate for this area."

Tempe was filled with fury. Not only because he'd bought a truck, but because of what the truck represented: the large gap between them. The fact that she struggled to pay the bills, and he'd purchased and had a truck delivered overnight to a remote address in Texas. The disparity between them had never been more obvious than it was at this moment. A wave of sadness drifted over her. They could never be together, even if she garnered enough courage to contemplate a relationship.

Her thoughts made her snappish. "I don't take charity."

He raised an aristocratic brow. "I didn't get it for you. It's for me."

His statement made her feel small, but instead of backing down, she struck out. "And we all know you enjoy the finer things in life." She wanted to call the words back as soon as they left her mouth, but she felt raw inside. It wasn't a feeling she was accustomed to. She didn't like that he made her feel that way.

"Well, as far as I can see, it was either purchase a truck or visit Thomas Hildebrand in the limo."

Tempe snapped her eyes at him. "If you'd bothered to ask, I was planning on riding horses, and for your future information, Aunt Effie has a car. We keep it in a building behind the house since she doesn't drive it very often."

Tempe glanced at the large black dually. Talk about nice! She'd always wanted one just like it. Knowing moneyman here, it was probably loaded.

He caught her staring at the truck.

"Come on, I know you want to ride in it."

At his teasing, the uneasy feeling subsided. She tilted her head and threw out a challenge. "Okay, you're on, but only if Kylo can come and I get to drive."

Without a qualm, he agreed. More points in his favor, not that she was keeping tabs. Eagerly she rounded the truck, called Kylo to her side and opened the driver's door. Kylo jumped in and made for the back seat, sitting on his haunches as if he owned the truck. She hoped he didn't slobber all over the really nice gray leather, but then shrugged. Trucks were built for life on the ranch.

Tempe grinned as she climbed in after him and her gaze was caught by the interior panel. She scanned all the goodies and rubbed her hands together. She hadn't been in a new vehicle, outside of the limo—and it didn't count—in ages. She inhaled deeply, breathing in the new truck smell, then started playing with the computer system. She might not have had a new vehicle in forever, but she was a pilot and well versed in all the latest technology.

Ewen cleared his throat. "Do you think we might begin our journey anytime soon?"

She grinned at him, turned the ignition and gassed the truck. His eyes widened and she put the dually in Drive. "Let's see what this baby's got," she said, then took off down the driveway. It didn't surprise her when Ewen gripped the armrest. Texas dust clouded behind the back tires until they reached the end of the drive and she turned left in the direction of Thomas's ranch.

"I take it you like the truck."

"Well, yeah, who wouldn't? It's a brand-new dually."

"I can think of a few people who wouldn't appreciate the finer offerings of this particular vehicle," he mumbled under his breath.

She glanced at him sharply before gluing her eyes back on the road. "You know, Scottie Boy, maybe you just need to find some new friends. Yours don't seem to appreciate the good things in life." She could have bitten out her tongue, because he was obviously referring to the women he dated in his real life. Women who dressed in silk and satin instead of the jeans and cowboy boots she pretty much lived in. Come to think of it, she couldn't even remember the last time she wore a dress, much less put on makeup, but she sternly reminded herself that she'd never allow another man to make her feel less than, due to her choices. The conversation took some of the joy out of driving the new truck.

"Did I misspeak?"

And just like that, Ewen's oh-so-proper word pulled her out of her funk. "Nah, just reminding myself of a few truths. Thanks for letting me drive your truck. It's really nice. I can hardly hear any road noise and the gadgets are way cool."

"I'm glad you're enjoying it, but something I said bothered you, and I'd like to know what it was."

Tempe shrugged. Now was as good a time as any to clear the air. "Listen, I appreciate all the help, and I know you're really only staying around because you're curious about the whole Scotland thing. I was just thinking that we come from two different worlds and we shouldn't be kissing or anything like that."

There! She'd cleared the air. When this was over, he could go back to his nice, comfy life, and she'd hopefully save the ranch and everything would be hunky-dory. Why, then, did she feel so bad after laying everything on the table?

She could feel his stare on her. "Is that the way you want it, Tempe?"

No! "Yes."

He gave a slight nod and stared out the passenger window. Gripping the steering wheel, Tempe thought about their short time together. Ewen was the first man she'd been attracted to since Riley was born. Was she going to pass on this opportunity due to—yes, she had to admit it—fear? Fear of giving up the independence and freedom she'd fought so hard to gain? Fear of getting hurt?

Her thoughts a riot of mixed emotions, she hadn't been as vigilant as she should have been, and she only had seconds to respond after she glanced in the rearview mirror.

"Ewen, hold on," she yelled right before she gave the steering wheel a hard jerk to the right.

Not again, Ewen thought as he gripped the armrest and braced himself. The dually's tires hit the side of the road, spitting gravel all the way up to his window. A large truck, one like theirs, if he wasn't mistaken, came up alongside them. He braced himself even more when he realized the other truck's intention. Metal on metal screeched as the other vehicle rammed the driver's side of their truck, trying to force them off the road. He closed his eyes and started praying.

"Oh no, you don't, you lily-livered coward! You'll pay for that."

Ewen opened his eyes in time to see Tempe jerk the steering wheel to the left and ram the opposing truck. He also spotted something somewhat alarming. "Uh, Tempe."

"Not now, Ewen. In case you didn't notice, I'm kinda busy here."

"I do understand, but there's a tractor trailer headed straight for us in the opposing lane."

Ewen was vastly relieved when Tempe's head jerked forward. Unfortunately, the truck trying to run them off the road must have seen the tractor trailer at the same time. The driver cut his truck toward theirs in order to avoid a head-on collision, and that had the effect of running them completely off the highway.

Ewen's neck snapped at the impact, but a second jolt at the front of the truck after they left the hardtop struck him even harder. His chest felt the restraint of the seat belt as they hit a sign that happened to be on the side of the road. His airbag exploded in his face right after he saw the other truck swerve into the right lane, missing the tractor trailer by mere inches. He couldn't even speak, and frantically tried to dig his brand-new pocketknife out of the pocket of his jeans to get rid of the airbag. His heart raced in fear. Was Tempe okay? Just as his fingers wrapped around the knife, his airbag suddenly deflated and Tempe was agitatedly running her hands all over his face.

"Ewen, are you okay? Does anything hurt?"

The questions, more than anything, told him Tempe wasn't injured. If she was, she certainly wouldn't be leaning over the console, checking him over. The rough pads of her fingers gently traced his face and neck and he closed his eyes because he'd never felt anything quite like the sensation—a touch of care, concern and maybe something else?

"Ewen, don't make me slap you awake."

Snapped out of his unrealistic musings, he popped his eyes open and spoke fast.

"I'm fine. Nothing's broken that I can tell. Let's get out of the truck and assess the damage, both to ourselves and the vehicle."

Ewen was almost drawn back into his musings at the look of worry on her face, but he shook his head and reached for the door handle. Once outside, he stood and checked all his limbs. A few bumps and bruises, but he was okay. Tempe came scrambling around the truck, Kylo on her heels, and propped her hands on her hips. Thankfully, she looked fine, but he wasn't happy about the bump on her forehead. The airbag should have prevented that, and he knew no one had messed with the vehicle because Ned's men had been on duty all night.

"I can't believe the nerve of that guy, trying to run us off the road like that. If it hadn't been for that tractor trailer, I could've gotten the best of him. If I'd caught him, maybe we could have gotten some answers."

Her cavalier attitude at the danger facing her and her family finally manifested itself into anger inside him. She could have been killed many times over, and she always went on the offense ready to take on any threat. It was commendable on one level, but at the moment it just made Ewen mad, maybe because the image of that tractor trailer bearing down on them was still fresh in his mind.

"Do you understand you could have been killed?" Her gaze snapped to his, but he couldn't seem to stop himself. "Do you always have to fight back every time, even when it may mean your life?" His words came out harsh, but he couldn't imagine a world without Tempe in it.

Tempe glanced at the brand-new dually, now scraped and dented almost beyond repair. "Oh, man, your truck. Ewen, I'm so sorry. I've ruined your beautiful truck."

Her statement felt like a fist to his chest. Was that what she thought? That he was worried about a stupid truck? Without thinking, he placed his hands on her shoulders and pulled her close, giving her time to stop him, then kissed her on the lips. Her indrawn breath almost made him pull back, but she wrapped her arms around his waist and kissed him back. Finally, his fear abated and he pulled away, staring into those green eyes of hers. They reminded him of a rare gem called chrysoberyl. It sparkled more than any other green stone in the world.

"Tempe—"

She pulled away before he could finish. "Ewen, it was just a kiss. Since we're both okay, we need to figure out how to get to Thomas's house. We still have to question him."

Of course, how could he forget. Tempe didn't want a relationship with anyone. She would never trust the male species, not even him, and that made him testy. "Don't worry about the truck. It's fully insured, and after it's repaired, it's yours."

When she opened her mouth, he knew what she was going to say, and he was irritated enough to get in a dig of his own. "Don't worry, it's not charity. I don't care to own a vehicle that's been wrecked." He knew his words hit their mark when her lips formed a straight, firm line, but he couldn't seem to stop himself. He sounded like a spoiled jerk, but she thought he was pampered anyway, so why not let her believe the worst?

Instead of arguing with him, she gave him a

jerky nod, called Kylo to her side, and got into the driver's seat of the truck. Ewen yanked his own door open and climbed in. The truck started with no problems. It might look like a train wreck, but it ran just fine. Probably because the thing was built like a tank.

Conversation was curtailed during the rest of the drive and Ewen was thankful, because he was trying to figure out why he'd reacted the way he had. Tempe didn't want a relationship, and neither did he. Why, then, did the thought of walking away when this was over feel wrong?

Tempe turned the dually into a long, paved driveway with manicured trees lining the way to the house. They circled a four-tiered water fountain and stopped in front of the house. Tempe sat there a minute after cutting the ignition.

"Ewen—"

He interrupted her before she could make platitudes about why she would never allow a man in her life. "Let's concentrate on Thomas Hildebrand."

She nodded and got out of the truck. He followed and they went up the steps leading to a missionary-style mini-mansion with a sandstone exterior. It was a beautiful property and Ewen admired the architecture, even if he didn't particularly care for the man living inside.

Ewen raised a hand to ring the doorbell, but

Tempe whipped around before his finger pressed the button. "Ewen, I need to tell you what I was doing in Scotland."

Now? She wanted to come clean on Hildebrand's doorstep? His heart hammered wildly in his chest. Would she finally tell him the truth? Was she finally ready to trust him? He lowered his arm and touched her cheek. "Tempe—"

The front door was flung open, and a woman stood there giving Tempe a shrewd look.

"Well, well, well, if it isn't little Tempe Calloway," she said.

"Mrs. Hildebrand. I'm sorry to intrude so early in the morning, but we need to speak to Thomas, if he's available."

The woman raised her arm. "Come on in."

As they entered, Thomas Hildebrand, dressed to the nines, quickly descended the long staircase.

"Tempe," Thomas greeted, affection in his voice, then a sharp nod to Ewen. "Mr. Duncan." A puzzled expression crossed his face and Ewen was of the opinion it was fake.

"I'm glad to see you, but this is an unexpected visit. I wish I had more time, but I have an appointment in an hour."

Tempe nodded briskly. "This won't take long. We'd like to talk to you about what's been happening at my ranch."

Thomas waved a hand toward a room down the

hall. "Why don't we step into my office?" They parted with his wife as they entered the room. Thomas seated himself behind a beautiful mahogany desk and motioned toward the chairs in front of the desk.

Ewen jumped in before Tempe had a chance to start firing questions. "Mr. Hildebrand, we appreciate you taking the time to see us."

He shook his head. "Mr. Duncan, I've known Tempe all her life. She's my neighbor and I was very good friends with her grandfather. I knew her parents, but Dillard, Dill Calloway, as everyone called him, was a unique character. I'm sure Tempe will agree he was both stubborn and crotchety, but everyone around here thought the world of him."

Tempe jumped in after giving Ewen a hard look, no doubt for trying to take the lead in the conversation. "Thomas," she said in a softer tone, "you know some of what's been going on at the ranch." He nodded. "Well, more things have happened. There've been several attempts on my life."

Thomas's head jerked toward Tempe, and Ewen studied him closely. He couldn't tell if the man's surprise was real or manufactured. He was running for governor soon, after all, and most politicians knew how to deflect and evade difficult topics.

"That's terrible, but I take it you weren't hurt?"

Tempe shook her head. "Listen, Thomas, the thing is, I want to know if my grandfather said anything to you before he died. Anything unusual."

Ewen silently applauded Tempe. She was savvier than he had given her credit for. She was using the soft approach to see if Thomas knew anything about the map and the gold. Good girl!

Thomas sat back in his oversize leather chair and steepled his fingers. "Is there a particular reason you ask that question?"

And then Tempe dropped a bombshell that impressed Ewen and would possibly trip Thomas up if he was involved. "We have reason to believe my grandfather was murdered."

EIGHTEEN

Back in the truck, on their way home, Tempe said, "No way could Thomas have faked that reaction. He turned green and looked like he was gonna puke. I don't think he knows anything about the map or the gold."

Pulling her eyes from the road, she stole a glance at Ewen. He had that imperious eyebrow raised at her language.

"What? I call 'em like I see 'em. The man almost fainted when I told him we suspect foul play."

Ewen laid his head back on the padded headrest and closed his eyes. Tempe still couldn't believe he was going to give her the truck, and she really shouldn't take it, but even wrecked, it was nicer than anything she owned. "Listen, Ewen, about the truck, you can get it fixed and it'll be good as new."

His eyes snapped open. "Forget the truck," he growled. "It's yours, and we have more important matters at hand." He paused a moment. "Before Hildebrand's wife answered the door, you were about to tell me why you were in Scotland."

Tempe was really hoping he'd forgotten her momentary lapse in judgment, but not Mr. James Bond. She doubted he ever missed a detail. If she was being truthful, she wanted him to trust her, but how could she ask that of him when she was withholding information. Should she tell him? Would he try to claim half the gold, or all of it?

Did it matter anymore? Had her grandfather forfeited his life for a map and possible gold? If she withheld the truth from Ewen, could more of her family members be hurt? With Ewen and Ned helping, she stood a chance of stopping this chaos. Nothing was more important than Riley, not a dumb map or the dream of enough gold to save the ranch, because without her daughter, she had nothing.

As the truck ate up the distance between Thomas's house and her ranch, a vivid memory passed through her mind. When she was small, they went to church regularly and she remembered the teacher in her Sunday school making them memorize verses. One came back to her very clearly. *One who is faithful in a very little is also faithful in much, and one who is dishonest in a very little is also dishonest in much.*

Was she being dishonest by not telling Ewen

what she was doing in Scotland? She found herself longing to get back to her roots and the church, everything her parents and grandfather had taught her. Not giving herself time to rethink it, she blurted out, "I went to Scotland to get the map."

"What?" He sounded perplexed.

She took a deep breath and explained the whole story. "After Granddad died and I found out about the map, well, it was several weeks after the funeral that I started looking for the book he'd hidden it in. Came to find out Aunt Effie had sold the few valuable books he owned to a bookstore in Texas to raise money to pay the bills. Somehow your grandfather found out about the book and called the store and bought it. The book store owner knew Granddad and he was kind enough to give me the buyer's name and address."

This was where it got sticky, but she plowed ahead with the truth. "I was afraid if you knew about the map, you'd claim finder's rights because your grandfather technically owned the book and the map inside it." She paused. "I know it's a murky area about who has legal rights to the map, but if it turns out there's really gold, I was hoping it would help save the ranch."

She gave him a quick glance, then cut her eyes back to the road, gripping the steering wheel hard. His frown didn't bode well.

"That's it? You flew to Scotland, completely changed your appearance and got a job under an assumed name to find a map your grandfather hid in a book that my grandfather bought?" He turned the full force of his sharp gaze on her, missing nothing. "Is that the truth, all of it?"

What? Here she'd just spilled all her secrets and he was acting like he didn't believe her? That burned. "You know what, Ewen? I don't care whether you believe me or not, because it's the truth. It's not fun to admit, but I was desperate enough to spend what little money I had for extras on a plane trip to Scotland to retrieve that map. I get that you've probably never been desperate a day in your life with all that money you've got socked away, but not all of us are so fortunate."

Dead silence filled the truck. When they pulled up in front of the ranch, she got out of the truck with Kylo bounding over the console behind her, then leaned back inside and said, "You know what, if you don't trust me, you can just go back where you came from." Slamming the truck door wasn't very satisfying as it was heavy-duty and only made a muffled noise.

As she marched toward the house, she heard Ewen exit the truck and come up behind her. He touched her arm and she spun around. His lack of trust in her hurt. Deeply. She hadn't allowed herself to care about anyone enough to get hurt since Riley was born, and nothing was going to change that.

"I'm not going anywhere."

She wanted him to leave, but another part of her wanted him to stay. She was torn and she didn't like it one bit. "Fine, let's get to the bottom of this and be done with it."

He winced at her words, but nodded. "I think we should look for the gold, and if we find it, set a trap. That will tell us if this is about the map and gold or something else entirely."

She nodded stiffly. "Fine." With Kylo right behind her, she turned and ran up the front steps, away from the confusing feelings Ewen evoked inside her. Chaos greeted her as soon as she stepped through the door. Simba taunted Kylo and they raced up the stairs. Liv met her at the door and opened her mouth to speak, but Tempe held up a hand and forestalled her.

"I assume everyone is congregated in the kitchen, based on the loud voices?" She frowned at Liv. "Were you nice to the grandparents?" Liv's mouth firmed and Tempe sighed. "Listen, sis, I need your help right now. Can you table the emotions until later, after things settle down?"

Liv's stubbornness turned to concern, and she hugged Tempe. "I'm sorry. It'll just take time to accept them," she whispered in Tempe's ear.

"But," she said as she released her, a bright smile filling her face, "I'll do it just for you."

Tempe studied her sister for a moment. "After this is all over, I want to know what's wrong." She held up a finger. "And don't deny it. I know you too well."

Liv nodded slowly. "Fine. I took a few days off from work, so tell me how I can help."

Ewen came through the door, but Tempe purposefully kept her eyes glued to Liv. Obviously catching the cold shoulder Tempe was giving Ewen, Liv shot Tempe that look—the one that meant Liv would grill Tempe later.

They entered the kitchen, and all eyes turned to Tempe. She stood there staring at everyone— Liv, her grandparents, Riley, Aunt Effie, Ewen's valet, Dudley, and Ned. Somehow this had become her family and she felt the heavy burden of responsibility. Almost as if he knew what she was feeling, Ewen moved close to her, but he didn't touch her. She appreciated the support, but she didn't want to get used to it, because as soon as this was over, he'd be out of her life for good.

"We questioned Thomas Hildebrand, and it's my opinion that he doesn't know anything about the gold." Before anyone could start asking questions, she went on. "Ewen came up with a plan and I think it's a good one. We're going to see if the gold is where I think it is, and if so, we'll set a trap. If someone comes after it, we'll catch who-ever's been systematically destroying the ranch. If no one comes, we'll keep investigating."

Tempe made eye contact with every person in the room except for Ewen. "I want all of you to listen to me, and listen good. Nothing—not gold or anything else—is worth any of my remaining family members getting hurt." Tempe took them all in. Minerva, along with Franklin, sitting there in borrowed clothes, determined to be a part of their family, Effie, a woman who had given up the best years of her life to help Tempe raise Riley, Liv, Tempe's stubborn, adorable, sister, and Riley, the wonderful child she'd been blessed with. Even Ewen's brother, Ned, was there. She'd give her life for any one of them. For the first time in years, Tempe choked on the emotion exploding through her.

Liv rolled her eyes, moved to the center of the room, and held her arms open. "If this is going to get mushy, we might as well have a group hug."

Tempe burst out laughing. Leave it to Liv to lighten the mood. Riley was the first into Liv's arms, and Liv boldly looked at Minerva and Franklin. "Come on, Gamy and PawPaw. You, too."

Tempe threw her arms in the air and joined in. It was an amazing experience, and some-thing broke loose in her…something that had been wound up tight for a long time. Her grin fell away and her heart did a flip when she looked over Liv's shoulder and saw Ewen leaning against the kitchen counter, a satisfied smile on his face.

In part, it was because of Ewen that she had allowed herself to open up enough to allow her grandparents into their lives. A warm glow spread through her body, but then she remembered he didn't believe her about her trip to Scotland, and the fuzziness evaporated.

Pulling away, she made an announcement. "Okay, Ewen and I are going to act like I'm checking on the stock, but we'll casually scout the location on the map." Everyone started talking at once and Tempe held up a hand for quiet. "It's too dangerous for anyone to go with us, and we won't go unless all of you agree to stay here under the watchful eye of Ned and his men."

There were grumblings, but everyone finally agreed. "I'll have two guys shadow us in case we run into trouble." She looked at Riley. "You know we'll be careful." Riley nodded gravely and Tempe smiled. "We'll be back before you know it."

Tempe whistled for Kylo to join them and Ewen followed her out the door, his emotions in complete turmoil. It was a blessing to watch Tempe's family heal, but the mistrust between him and

Tempe stole some of the satisfaction. They made their way to the old shack holding the worn-out equipment and swiftly saddled their perspective horses. Ewen took firm control of Bronco this time and Tempe hooked a foot into Masie's stirrup, mounting the horse in one smooth move. The woman was poetry in motion.

"Tempe, I—"

"Not now, Ewen. We can talk when this is over."

He really didn't know what to say anyway, because no one in their right mind would spend the last of their money chasing a map that possibly might never lead to anything. Ewen didn't know anything except what Tempe had told him about her grandfather. For all he knew, the man could have had dementia before he died and the whole map and gold thing was a way to entertain Riley. But why, then, did he make it seem so real upon his death, leaving Tempe to chase a dream. Well, they'd know soon enough.

Tempe had brought her shotgun, which she'd shoved into a saddle holster, and Ewen still had the pistol he'd slipped into his pocket before they visited Thomas Hildebrand. He couldn't see Ned's men, but he knew they were close. Nevertheless, he scanned the area as the horses moved forward. They were sitting ducks for a sharpshooter.

"So where do you think the gold is?"

Tempe kept her gaze forward. "Based on the

map tableau, it's in one of the foothill caves. Riley and I searched several of the caves, but there's hundreds of them. You'd have to know exactly where you're looking to find something. It's a great hiding place."

"Tell me about your grandfather."

She gave him an icy look. "He was of sound mind."

"I didn't say he wasn't. I just want to know about him. He sounds like an interesting character."

Her tense shoulders relaxed, and that, in turn, made him relax. She even smiled, and satisfaction filled him at having made that happen.

She stared into the distance. "He was stubborn and crotchety and we—me, Liv, Riley and Effie—loved him to pieces. After Mom and Dad died, he didn't even take time to grieve because he and Effie had two devastated girls to console and take care of. I was seventeen and Liv was nineteen at the time." She went quiet for a moment and Ewen let her gather her thoughts.

"He was from a time of the past, when people said what they meant and meant what they said. He was an original cowboy in every aspect. Tough as an old bird."

She swallowed hard, but Ewen stayed quiet. "I just never thought of him dying. He was one of those people full of life every minute of the day." She swallowed again. "He always said he'd make good use of the days God had given him, and when it was his time to go, well, only God knew that."

Her mood changed in an instant. "I hope God took into account someone who might've taken my grandfather before it was his time to go."

Ewen didn't know what to say to that, except, "Tempe, if someone did take your grandfather before his time, we'll find them and justice will be served."

They'd reached the mountains and Tempe stopped Masie and slid off the horse. "We're on foot from here. Kylo, stay with the horses."

Ewen stared up at what Tempe referred to as a foothill and frowned. "I was thinking more along the lines of a hill. You know, a small mound."

Tempe laughed again and his traitorous heart soared. "Come on, Scottie Boy, we've got a little climbing to do."

"Do we need ropes?"

She laughed again, which was what he was going for. The climb really didn't look too bad. He got off his horse and followed Tempe. At the base of the foothill, she pointed up. "According to the map, the gold should be right up there."

Ewen looked up but only saw rock with scrub brush growing out the side of it. He scrambled after Tempe as she placed one foot into a toehold and started pulling herself up. They were about halfway up the hill when Tempe reached a rather bushy spot on the side. She fought with the scrub brush for a minute, then looked down and breathed excitement. "There's a cave up here. This has to be it."

He caught her enthusiasm and kept climbing. She disappeared for a moment, but stuck her hand down when he reached the top of the incline. He pushed himself up and followed her into a small cave, large enough to stand up in, but shallow. It didn't extend deeper into the foothill.

Pulling out his phone, he turned on the light and scanned the walls, floor and ceiling. He'd expected something a little, well, more. He'd toured caves in the past and had seen extraordinary things. Small pools of water and beautiful stalagmites, but all this hole in the wall held was dust and dirt and stone walls. He spotted one small wet spot that appeared to be water in the corner, but that was it.

"Well, this won't be one for the tourists." He was trying to ease their tension, but all he got in return from Tempe was a grumpy "humph."

"Let's start at the entrance and make our way left. We'll check every nook and cranny in the cave."

Ewen prayed they'd find gold. It would help Tempe save her ranch, and that would be one problem solved. They checked every crevice as they made their way around, from top to bottom, but they didn't find anything. When they got back to the entrance, Tempe propped her hands on her hips and stared at the inside of the cave. "We may never find it in here. I wonder why he hid it? Maybe he knew there was danger associated with the gold and he buried it for safekeeping until the danger was resolved."

Ewen wanted this so bad for her, but he was afraid they weren't going to find any gold. They shifted dirt with their boots, but the cave was mostly rock. There weren't many places to bury something. They checked for another forty-five minutes to no avail. Tempe finally sat on a rocky outcropping and looked at him with defeat in her eyes.

"There isn't any gold, is there?"

NINETEEN

Deep down, Tempe had always wondered if the gold was too good to be true, but she'd wanted it so badly. Everything in her life had always been tough, but she'd managed. She'd had to fight her way into the Blue Angels. She'd learned how to be a single mother. Losing her parents at such a vulnerable age had been hard, but now… They'd have to sell the cattle during the October-November sale because they couldn't afford to feed them until the spring sale, when prices would be at their highest. They just might lose the ranch, and she refused to allow Minerva and Franklin to bail them out.

But first things first. She stood with more bravado than she felt. "Well, I guess that's it, then. But if there's no gold, then why the destruction of my property? And don't say it's someone in the Blue Angels, because they don't have enough to gain if they got caught committing a felony."

"But what if whoever is committing these vile acts thinks there's gold?"

That snapped Tempe out of her despair. "What?" Ewen smiled and Tempe's heart skipped a beat.

"They may not be aware there's no gold, only that there's a map supposedly leading to the gold. And Tempe, what if we have the wrong cave? We can scout out other caves and keep searching."

Her heart melted a little at the offer, but she'd spent enough time and money chasing a dream. "No, this is the exact spot on the map. I want to know that my family's safe before I finish my last three months with the Angels, and I have a limited amount of time to do that. We need to flush out whoever is doing this."

"Okay, I'm hoping someone followed us today and will come to the cave tonight. We'll be waiting when that happens."

"Fine. Let's get out of here."

They climbed back down the hill and mounted their horses, Tempe with a heavy heart. Kylo practiced his herding on the horses and neither one of them said anything until they were close to the house.

"Everyone is going to be so disappointed there's no gold."

"Tempe, let me help you. I have more money than I can spend in a lifetime."

Acid churned in her stomach at the offer and she lashed out, "You don't even believe my explanation about my time in Scotland. Why would you offer money to someone you don't trust? I don't need your money and I don't need your God. I'll figure out how to save the ranch the way I've always done, by myself."

He frowned at her, but she'd had enough and the loss of the possibility of finding gold was the last straw. Bart met them as they rode into the yard and took Tempe's reins. "Y'all go on in. I'll take care of the critters."

"Thanks, Bart."

Without saying a word to Ewen, Tempe girded herself for the disappointment waiting inside for her. She bounded up the steps, Kylo on her heels. Everyone with the exception of Ned had crowded into the foyer, hopeful expressions on their faces.

"Mama, did you find the gold. Are we rich?" Riley said, her young voice pulling deeply on Tempe's heartstrings. Opening her arms, Tempe closed her eyes as Riley flew into them. She released Riley and stepped back, looking at each loving face in turn.

"There's no gold." Everyone started talking at once and Tempe held up a hand, asking for quiet. "But it doesn't matter. We'll get by. We always have."

Tempe heard Minerva mumble, "I have plenty

of money, but someone I know is too proud to take it." Tempe chose to ignore that statement. Minerva was probably right about Tempe's pride, and she would have to think about that, but not right now.

"But I have some good news." Everyone quieted at that statement. "Ewen hopes someone followed us where we went today and will try to get to the gold tonight if they believe it's there. We'll be waiting for them."

Tempe turned toward the stairs. "I'm going to my room to clean up and rest. It'll be a long night."

Effie stepped forward, loving concern in her eyes. "Tempe, you and Ewen missed lunch. Why don't you eat before you rest?"

Tempe's stomach churned at the thought of food and she forced a smile. "Maybe later."

She trudged up the steps, and once in her room, leaned against the door and closed her eyes. She castigated herself for spending what little money they had on that trip to Scotland. Of course, if she hadn't gone, she would never have met Ewen.

She opened her eyes and pushed herself away from the door. Not that it mattered. There were a lot of things she really liked about Ewen, and for a while there, she...not that it mattered now. He didn't believe her, and she couldn't get interested in a man. A heavy burden weighed on her shoulders as she went to the bathroom. Maybe she wouldn't ever be able to trust a man again.

Splashing water on her face and drying it with a towel, she stared at herself in the mirror. In the past, whenever she got down, a good, stern speech to herself had helped buoy her spirits, but all she felt right now was weariness.

Moving back to the bedroom, she decided to take a nap, but came to a halt when she saw who was in her room. "Minerva?"

The older woman moved to stand right in front of her. Her eyes shifted away, and Tempe blew out a sigh. "Out with it, Minerva. What's on your mind?"

The previously haughty woman clasped both her hands in front of her and raised her head. Tempe was surprised to see what amounted to a plea in her eyes.

"Tempe, I know you won't take money from us, but, well…"

Getting impatient, Tempe said, "Just spit it out."

The haughtiness came back in spades. "Fine! Franklin and I want to be part of this family." She took a deep breath. "We'd like to purchase a hundred acres from you and build a house on the ranch. We want to be close to you, Olivia and Riley. The money from the sale of the land would also help you pay your bills. And don't worry, you'll inherit the land back when we pass on."

Well, this was a surprise. Tempe wasn't sure she wanted Minerva and Franklin in her hip pocket all the time.

Minerva responded to her hesitation with a smile. "Don't worry, we won't be here all the time, just for visits." She gave Tempe a sly look. "We're coming for visits anyway. At least if we have our own home here, we won't be underfoot in your house."

Tempe gave her a hard look. "Is your change of heart for real?"

Minerva didn't balk at the question. "Fair enough. The answer is yes. When you become our age, your priorities change."

Tempe could understand that and she held out a hand. "Deal. We'll have a Realtor determine what the property is worth and that'll be the price."

A smile bloomed on Minerva's face, and if Tempe still had any reservations, that removed all doubt. It was obvious the woman was pleased and excited.

"You won't regret this, Tempe. I'll let you get some rest now," she said and left the room, quietly closing the door behind her. Fully clothed, Tempe lay down on her bed, thinking of everything that had happened over the last few days. She also thought of the money they would get upon the sale of property to her grandparents. They just might make it after all…

Tempe woke with a start and raised her head to glance out the window. They had about an hour and a half before dusk, when she and Ewen would make their way to the cave. She hopped out of bed and went to the bathroom to comb her hair and splash water on her face.

She decided to take a walk and clear the cobwebs before they went on their nighttime excursion to the cave. Leaving her bedroom, she only met Effie as she popped her head out of the kitchen.

"In case Liv comes down, tell her I'm taking a walk before we leave for the cave later. Don't worry, Ned's men are stationed everywhere. I'll be safe enough close to the house."

Effie nodded and disappeared back into the kitchen. Tempe opened the front door, took a deep breath and moved forward with purpose. She had to get herself back on track. They would discover who was systematically destroying the ranch, and who wanted her dead. If not tonight, then soon.

She looked at the burned barn. They'd have to get the debris cleaned up soon. She meandered around several of the outbuildings but stilled when something cold touched the back of her neck. "Don't move, or I'll shoot you where you stand."

* * *

Ewen had decided to take a rest himself, but the sun was descending and it was time for him and Tempe to make their way to the cave. They needed to get there early and take positions before the perpetrators, hopefully, arrived. He dressed, then slipped into the facilities at the end of the hall. After tidying up a bit, he went down the stairs and into the kitchen where Effie appeared to be cleaning up after dinner.

"Ewen, would you like something to eat before you and Tempe leave?" Effie offered.

She smiled, but there was an underlying sadness. Ewen had prayed before his nap that God would somehow help Tempe manage to hold on to the ranch. She was too proud to accept help and he didn't know what to do.

"Nothing to eat, but I'll take a cup of coffee." He took a chair and stared at the whole household, who were staring back at him. The kitchen was obviously a popular place. Riley was staring the hardest, a miniature image of her mother.

"Riley, is something wrong?"

She peered up at him with big green eyes. "Are you going to be my new dad?"

Minerva gasped and that gave Ewen time to recover from the disconcerting question. "Riley, what makes you ask that?"

Those big green eyes, so much like her mother's, narrowed. It was even more disconcerting.

"'Cause I saw you kissin' Mama in the yard when y'all came back from Mr. Hildebrand's house, and people who kiss get married." The last was said with obstinacy, as if Riley was judge and jury.

Ewen didn't quite know how to respond, and was saved when Effie peered out the kitchen window.

"Tempe should be back in by now."

His discomfort dissolved in an instant. "Where did she go?" His tone must have been sharp, because Effie frowned at him.

"She went for a walk to clear her head, but that was an hour ago. She should be back by now."

Ewen had to rein in his fear by reminding himself that Ned's men were outside and Tempe was a responsible adult, but then her daring stunts in the helicopter and jet came to mind, and the fear returned, twofold.

He pulled out his cell phone.

"What'cha doing?" Riley asked, sliding off her chair and moving close to his side.

Those big green pools in her eyes were filled with innocence and a touch of anxiety. In that moment, Ewen decided that no matter what transpired between him and Tempe, he would figure out a way to save Tempe's ranch.

"I'm going to find your mother."

Riley's eyes lit with interest and she glanced at the phone. "How ya gonna do that?"

Ewen grinned. "Unbeknownst to your mother, I placed a tracking device on her yesterday." He held up his phone. "See this small picture, now watch." Ewen tapped the app and a tracking screen popped up. "The red dot will be your mother, but it'll take a few seconds to find her location. I also placed one on you."

"Yeah, where?" She tilted her head to one side. "You talk funny, you know that?"

"Yes," he answered bemusedly, "I've been told that. Now, look right inside your boot, near the top." Ewen grinned when she bent over and pulled her boot off. She examined the inside of her boot, then whooped after she located the tiny device and held it in the air.

"I found it."

"You sure did. Now put it back for the moment so I can find you if you get lost."

She carefully placed it back in her boot, slipped it back on and stared at him the way only children can. "So's you can find me anywhere?"

He grinned and nodded. "Anywhere in the world. The tracking devices are fed by satellite."

His phone pinged and Ewen looked down. At first, he didn't comprehend what he was seeing, because it made no sense, but when the reality of it hit him, he immediately called Ned. In a grim voice, he said, "Meet me outside. Now."

Riley's eyes had rounded with moisture. "Is my mama okay?"

Tamping down his own fear, he forced a smile. "Of course, she is. I'll bring her back to you. I promise." And he meant it. No one was going to hurt Tempe.

Riley must have believed him. She gave a tight nod and firmed her lips, so much like her mother. Ewen wanted to grab her and give her a big hug of reassurance, but before he could contemplate that action, she flung herself into his arms and grabbed him around the waist.

"Thank you, Mr. Ewen."

And just like that, Ewen fell in love with Tempe's young daughter. Determined to get to her mother in time, he gave her a tight hug and pulled away, his hands on her thin shoulders.

"Don't worry, Riley, we'll be back soon."

He looked around the room and spotted the dog. "Kylo, stay with Riley!"

Seeing the concerned faces sitting around the big old kitchen table, Ewen decided it was time to come clean with these people who were beginning to mean so much to him. "Just so you know, I'm not without training for these types of situations. I'm a novelist, yes, but I'm also an analyst for the Defense Intelligence Agency, working for the United States government. I'll bring Tempe back."

He left the house amid an outburst of chatter, determined to find Tempe alive and well. There were too many unresolved matters between them.

TWENTY

Tempe couldn't believe it. The answer had been in front of them the whole time, but based on the information they had gathered, neither she nor Ewen would ever have figured out who was destroying her property and trying to kill her.

After she'd felt the cold barrel of a pistol against the back of her neck, she'd done exactly as she was told. She'd moved forward through the woods that led out to a road where two saddled horses were waiting.

Both of them mounted, but Patricia Hildebrand had a gun pointed at Tempe and ordered her to lead the way to the location on the map. The sky was continuing to darken and Tempe kept trying to figure a way out of this, but she also wanted answers. When they were ten minutes or so from the cave, she started asking questions, calmly so as to keep Patricia steady.

"So you know about the map?"

The woman gave a cynical laugh. "Of course,

I know about the map. That stupid map! Your grandfather told Thomas all about it."

Tempe didn't want to upset the woman, possibly causing her to shoot, so she spoke slowly. "Listen, there is no gold. The map led us to a cave and there's nothing there."

Patricia scoffed. "Oh, there's gold all right. I figured you'd found the location when you and that man came to visit Thomas, and you just confirmed my suspicions. Your stubborn grandfather would never tell Thomas where it was." Her voice turned sly and Tempe got a sinking feeling. "I talked Thomas into offering to buy your ranch years ago because we needed the money, but the old man refused to sell."

That didn't make sense. "But you don't need our ranch or the gold. You inherited plenty of family money and Thomas's ranch seems to be doing well."

Patricia gave a haughty sniff. "Our lifestyle is very expensive, and it took a good chunk of my inheritance to pull Thomas's ranch out of the red. Now I've convinced him to run for governor and we need to fill his war chest."

Tempe slowly processed everything Patricia was saying, all the time waiting for an opportunity to turn the tables. "That's what fundraisers are for."

"I'll not lower myself to begging for money

and I *will* be the governor's wife. I've certainly put up with enough from that man. It's the least he can do for me."

Tempe spoke very carefully now, feeling the tension rolling off Patricia in waves. Her suspicions were growing by leaps and bounds and she had to stay calm. "My grandfather would never have sold the ranch. He wanted to keep it in the family." It was a baited question and Patricia fell for it.

"Don't you think I knew that," she snapped. "If the old man had sold, I wouldn't have had to take extreme measures. It's all his fault."

A cloud of darkness and fury fell over Tempe as she slowly asked, "What extreme measures, Patricia?"

"I had to get rid of him, of course."

And there it was. Tempe's grandfather had been murdered. Her hands tightened on the horse's reins. She wanted to jump off her horse and strangle the woman.

Patricia trilled a laugh. "That stupid old man. He was stubborn to the end. Wily, too. I assumed you would sell if he was out of the way, but I was wrong." Anger entered her voice. "You're as stubborn as he was, but after you're gone, the ranch will have to be sold."

That answered one question. Patricia didn't intend for Tempe to make it out of this alive, but

Tempe had too much to live for. There was Riley; Tempe would face death a thousand times and survive because her daughter needed her. The loss that Patricia so casually spoke of was like a fist to Tempe's chest, and she breathed deeply to remain calm. And Ewen—Tempe just now realized how much she...loved him? Impossible! She hadn't even known him that long, but there it was, a big warm glow positioned right in the middle of her heart. She loved Scottie Boy. She wasn't going to die; she'd make sure of it.

"Patricia, it sounds like you're going to kill me anyway and I'd like to know if you used someone in the Blue Angels to sabotage my jet." It was another fishing expedition, but Patricia took the bait.

"My dear, I have connections you can't even begin to imagine. I hired an expert to handle the problem. After making sure he had proper credentials, he posed as a deliveryman and slipped on base. He knew all about planes and had no problem making sure yours wouldn't land."

Tempe was vastly relieved to know there wasn't a traitor within the Blue Angels ranks.

"But if you didn't know the location of the gold, why try to kill me? You were taking a chance on never finding the gold. And I'd like to know if Sheriff Brady was involved."

Patricia huffed. "That old fool! No, the sheriff knows nothing. I tried to scare you into getting rid of the ranch, but I finally realized you'd never willingly give it up, so I decided to get rid of you, buy your ranch for pennies on the dollar and take my chances on finding the map myself."

"If you're short on funds, how were you planning to buy my ranch?"

"I still have money, but I need more, and numerous banks would be honored to give someone of my stature a loan."

It was time for a different tack. "Why not just take the gold? You don't need the ranch."

That laugh again. "Let's go to the cave. Then you'll understand."

"One more question. Does your husband know what you've been up to?"

Patricia sniffed. "No, he's a fool, too. If it weren't for me, he wouldn't even be running for governor."

By then they had arrived at the foothill and Tempe pointed upward. "It's up there." There was no way Patricia could climb and hold a gun on her.

The woman studied the situation for a moment, then pointed the gun at Tempe. "You'll go first and stay back when I get up there. If you try anything, one of us will die, and if it's you, I'll make sure Riley doesn't have anyone left to take care of her. She'll end up in a foster home."

Grimly, Tempe nodded and slid off her horse. She'd have to watch for a sure opening because no way was Riley going to be orphaned. And Ewen—she wanted a chance to tell him how she felt. It didn't matter that he didn't believe her. She'd convince him to trust her *when* she got out of this alive. For the first time in years, she took a deep breath and opened her heart to God. As soon as she started praying, it came to her that she hadn't ever quit believing; she'd only been angry. As she prayed, a peace and warmth she hadn't felt in a long time spread through her mind and body.

Placing one foot in a crevice, she started climbing and prayed the whole way. It felt so wonderful she never wanted to stop. She wasn't alone anymore. She couldn't believe she'd allowed her anger to become an obstacle between her and the Almighty, but He was with her now and she intended to keep it that way.

She reached the cave in a short time. Backing away from the entrance, she allowed Patricia to follow her up. It was too dangerous to go for the gun at the ledge. Patricia pulled the weapon from the back of her waistband and motioned Tempe to sit on the dirt floor.

"Patricia, there's no gold here. Ewen and I looked everywhere."

"Shut up," she said as she pulled out a flashlight with her other hand.

Patricia searched the small cave, keeping the gun trained on Tempe all the time, and Tempe stayed quiet. A sound of satisfaction purred from Patricia's throat as she placed a hand on the wet area, then brought it to her nose.

"What is it?" Tempe asked. A riot of emotions threatened to spill out, curiosity being one of them.

Patricia's lips twisted into a semblance of a smile. "Gold. Liquid gold."

It took a minute for Tempe to assimilate what she was talking about, and then it hit her square between the eyes. "Oil?" she breathed.

"Yes. Oil shale. A bit more expensive to extricate, but worth a lot of money all the same." Patricia raised the pistol and pointed it straight at Tempe's head. "And now it's time for you to meet your Maker."

Before Patricia could pull the trigger, the sound of a helicopter resonated in the small cave and Tempe took full advantage of the momentary distraction.

Ewen silently willed Ned to fly the helicopter faster. He was thankful his brother had thought to have one hidden and available on the ranch, because otherwise, they may have been too late. Two of Ned's men had accompanied them.

They approached the cave Tempe and he had

visited, and his heart climbed into his throat when he saw two people struggling, balanced on the edge of the small cliff.

"Get closer, get closer," he yelled. They all had headsets on, and Ned, sitting beside him in the pilot's seat, nodded grimly. He swung the chopper close to the foothill and Ewen got a good look. "What!?" was all he could say when he spotted Tempe struggling with Patricia Hildebrand for possession of a pistol. Thomas Hildebrand's wife? She was the culprit in all of this?

The women twisted around, and Tempe's back faced the drop-off. It was in that moment Ewen realized how much Tempe meant to him. He had fallen in love with the independent, strong-willed, courageous woman. He couldn't lose her now. Not before he had a chance to tell her that he believed her, believed in her. Ewen swallowed hard and spoke low. "Ned, I love that woman. She's your future sister-in-law."

Ned, very much a risk-taker like Tempe, turned his head and grinned. "Then let's go save her." He banked the helicopter away from the foothill and gave instructions to one of his men. "John, when we swing back around, see if you can get a shot."

"Yes, sir!"

Ewen glanced at the back seat. John, wearing a secure harness, leaned out the side of the helicopter, raising his rifle with a steady hand.

"Not a kill shot," Ned said.

"Understood, sir!" John barked back.

When they were in position, Ned held the chopper in the air and Ewen watched with a feeling of total helplessness. There was nothing he could do. The two women struggled, and Tempe finally twisted their positions. Tempe was now on the inside of the ledge. A muffled sound came from the back of the chopper and everything seemed to happen in slow motion as blood bloomed on Patricia's left arm. She fell away from Tempe and teetered on the edge of the drop-off for what seemed like forever. Just as she started falling, she pointed the gun, still in her hand, at Tempe, and Ewen heard the report of the gun being fired.

Patricia fell off the small cliff and Tempe fell backward simultaneously. "Set the chopper down! Set the chopper down!" Ewen screamed into the mic. He hopped onto the ground before the helicopter was stabilized and ran to the base of the hill. His hands shook as he placed his foot in a toehold and tried to grab onto a piece of rock to pull himself up. He prayed as he climbed. Tempe couldn't be dead. A woman so full of life and courage and daring had to survive. He propelled himself over the ledge and squatted beside her. Swallowing the bile that had climbed into his throat, he placed a finger on her neck and heaved a sigh of relief when he felt a strong heartbeat.

The blood seeping through her clothes on her shoulder upset him, but she was alive.

"Ewen?" Tempe groaned and tried to sit up.

He gently held her down. "No, don't get up. We need to get you checked out."

Tempe, being Tempe, nudged his hand away and pushed herself into a sitting position, reached to the back of her head, then checked her shoulder.

Ewen couldn't contain his feelings any longer, and when he opened his mouth, it felt right. Everything felt right. "Tempe, I think, well, that is, I'm sure—"

"For a man with such an extensive vocabulary, you sure are having a hard time of it. Just say it."

"I love you," he blurted out.

Those green eyes that had reflected so many emotions were now filled with something he'd never seen before, right before they lit with amusement. "Well, that's good. I'm glad I don't have to follow you to Scotland to make you admit it."

"When I thought you might die, I knew, I just knew… What did you say?"

"Come 'ere, Scottie Boy." He moved closer and she placed both hands on the sides of his face. "I love you, too. We'll work everything else out, where we'll live and all that, but right now we need to see what happened to Patricia, and then I have something to show you."

She got to her feet and Ewen tried to stop her, but she waved a negligent hand in the air. "I'm fine. The shoulder is a flesh wound. I've had worse."

They both stared at the spot where Patricia fell, then he took her by the arm. "Ned will see to Patricia. What do you want to show me?"

She nodded, motioned him into the cave and pointed to the wet spot he'd noticed on their previous visit. "There's the gold."

"I don't understand."

Tempe laid her hand on the wet spot, then raised it to his nose. "Oil, Ewen, the gold isn't gold as we thought of it. It's an oil shale buried beneath this foothill, seeping through the rock."

Astounded, he bent down and looked at the wet spot and placed his own hand on it. Tempe was right. He grinned as he looked up at her. "You'll be a rich woman. You'll be able to save the ranch."

For the first time since he'd known her, her lips trembled. "At what cost? Patricia Hildebrand told me she murdered my grandfather." Her lips stilled then slowly curved at both corners. "But if she's still alive after that fall, she'll spend the rest of her life in jail."

Ewen stared at the phone she pulled out of her pocket.

"I recorded her confession."

Ewen stood and enfolded her in his arms, brushed his lips against her temple, and whispered in her ear. "You're an amazing woman, Tempe Calloway. Let's get out of here."

They climbed down and walked over to where Ned and the other two men were standing over Patricia. Ned looked at them without an ounce of pity in his eyes.

"She's conscious and angry. We're field-trained in emergency situations, so we can rig up a gurney and take her to the hospital. We'll notify the police on the way."

After calling the house and assuring the family Tempe was okay, Ewen took her by the arm and led her to the horses. "Are you able to ride?" he gently asked Tempe. She nodded and he said to Ned, "We'll take the horses in, and thanks for everything."

His brother gave him a salute, and Ewen and Tempe mounted the horses and started the ride back to the ranch. He was glad she was able to ride because he wanted some privacy before they got back to the house and this was a good opportunity to talk. When they were away from the chopper, he tried to figure out where to start.

"Just spit it out, Ewen. I know you've got secrets, but—" she paused "—if this relationship thing is going to work, we can't have that."

He went straight to the point. "I'm in the DIA."

She whipped her head around. "What? For the United States government?"

"Yes. I collect and analyze intelligence on foreign militaries, and—"

"I know what the DIA does." She seemed to ponder his bald statement. "It all makes sense now. You do write books, but it's a perfect cover for your other job."

"Exactly!" He was relieved she understood. Now for the hard part. "Tempe, I know we've only known each other a short time, but will you marry me?" She fidgeted in her saddle and he snapped, "I'm not like Riley's father. I love you and I love her. I'll never leave you in the lurch."

She looked away and his heart sunk. She was a risk-taker; would she take a risk on them?

"Okay," came the quiet reply.

He wanted to make sure he heard her correctly. "Is that a yes?"

She flashed fiery green eyes at him. "I love you and I said I'd marry you, okay?"

Not the sweet, heartfelt answer he was hoping for, but he grabbed onto it with both hands. "We'll marry in Scotland, but if you're happy on the ranch, we can make that our home base."

"We'll get married after I finish my tour with the Blue Angels," she declared.

Ewen grinned and prodded Bronco forward. His life wasn't going to be smooth and perfect, but it certainly was going to be interesting, and he wouldn't have it any other way.

* * * * *

*If you enjoyed this story, don't miss
Liz Shoaf's next suspenseful romance,
available later this year
from Love Inspired Suspense!*

*Find more great reads at
www.LoveInspired.com*

Dear Reader,

The name for the heroine in *Texas Ranch Sabotage* came from an unusual circumstance. Sadly, I attended a funeral for one of my uncles. A bulletin listed all the names of the immediate family, and I spotted a name I'd never seen before: Tempe Shoaf. I asked Mom about this woman. Who was she? Why didn't I know anything about her? All she could remember was that Tempe died as a baby. In all these years, no one had mentioned her to me, and I started wondering what she would have been like and if the dynamics of the family would have been different had she lived.

In *Texas Ranch Sabotage*, the dynamics of Tempe's family change and they heal after a long and arduous journey. I hope you enjoy Tempe and Ewen's story along with his spoiled cat, Simba, and her cattle-dog-in-training, Kylo. Love is in the air, Texas style!

Liz Shoaf

Get 4 FREE REWARDS!

We'll send you 2 FREE Books <u>plus</u> 2 FREE Mystery Gifts.

THE BELL TOLLS

Death and a Pot of Chowder
CORNELIA KIDD

Worldwide Library books feature gripping mysteries from "whodunits" to police procedurals and courtroom dramas.

FREE Value Over **$20**

Visit
ReaderService.com
Today!

As a valued member of the Harlequin Reader Service, you'll find these benefits and more at ReaderService.com:

- Try 2 free books from any series
- Access risk-free special offers
- View your account history & manage payments
- Browse the latest Bonus Bucks catalog

Don't miss out!

If you want to stay up-to-date on the latest at the Harlequin Reader Service and enjoy more content, make sure you've signed up for our monthly News & Notes email newsletter. Sign up online at ReaderService.com or by calling Customer Service at 1-800-873-8635.